HUNT FOR THE BAMBOO RAT

Also by Graham Salisbury

Blue Skin of the Sea
Lord of the Deep
Night of the Howling Dogs

PRISONERS OF THE EMPIRE BOOKS
Eyes of the Emperor
House of the Red Fish
Under the Blood-Red Sun

FOR YOUNGER READERS
The Calvin Coconut Series

GRAHAM SALISBURY

HUNT FOR THE BAMBOO RAT

EMBER

Text copyright © 2014 by Graham Salisbury
Cover art copyright © 2014 by Jon Valk
Map copyright © 2014 by Joe LeMonnier

All rights reserved. Published in the United States by Ember, an imprint of Random House Children's Books, a division of Penguin Random House LLC, New York. Originally published in hardcover in the United States by Wendy Lamb Books, an imprint of Random House Children's Books, New York, in 2014.

Ember and the E colophon are registered trademarks of Penguin Random House LLC.

Visit us on the Web! randomhouseteens.com

Educators and librarians, for a variety of teaching tools,
visit us at RHTeachersLibrarians.com

The Library of Congress has cataloged the hardcover edition of this work as follows:
Hunt for the bamboo rat / by Graham Salisbury. — First edition.
pages cm
Summary: Zenji Watanabe, seventeen, is sent from Hawaii to the Philippines to spy on the Japanese during World War II and, after he is captured and tortured, must find a way to survive months of being lost in the jungle behind enemy lines.
ISBN 978-0-375-84266-5 (hardback) — ISBN 978-0-375-94070-5 (lib. bdg.) — ISBN 978-0-307-97970-4 (ebook) [1. Spies—Fiction. 2. Prisoners of war—Fiction. 3. Survival—Fiction. 4. Japanese Americans—Fiction. 5. World War, 1939–1945— Philippines—Fiction. 6. Philippines—History—Japanese occupation, 1942–1945— Fiction.] I. Title.
PZ7.S15225Hun 2014
[Fic]—dc23
2014005743

ISBN 978-0-375-84267-2 (trade pbk.)

Printed in the United States of America

First Ember Edition 2015

Random House Children's Books supports the First Amendment and celebrates the right to read.

In honor of
Lieutenant Commander
Henry Forester Graham, USN
Killed in Action 1945
Japan

CHINATOWN

Zenji Watanabe was in the middle of an early-morning daydream as he walked to his job at Honolulu Harbor. He was trying to imagine himself as a Buddhist priest like his teachers at Japanese school when a rat leaped out of a garbage can just ahead, sending the metal lid clanging to the sidewalk.

He jumped back and adjusted his glasses. "Crazy rat!"

Late for work, he was cutting through Chinatown, hoping he could make it without any trouble.

But the rat changed that.

Three Chinese guys sitting on their heels two blocks down looked his way.

"Oh, man," Zenji whispered.

It was August 1941, and in Honolulu tensions between the

Chinese and Japanese had risen like fire-spewing dragons because of what had happened in Nanking, China. In 1937, the Imperial Japanese Army killed over a hundred thousand innocent Chinese civilians. Maybe even more. To Zenji it was a tragedy. But some patriotic Japanese immigrants had publicly cheered Japan's success. Anger at Japan still smoldered in Chinatown.

The three guys were about his age, seventeen. They seemed as surprised to see him as he was to see them.

One guy had hair that hung past his shoulders. "Hey!" He sprang to his feet.

The others got up, shooting Zenji dirty looks.

Zenji pretended not to see them, and turned casually down the street to his left. The second he was out of sight, he ran.

Hide—an open door, a dark alley, a low window!

Where?

He spotted a rusted fire escape and climbed it, hoping it would hold. One floor up, he punched through a window screen and tumbled into somebody's bedroom.

He scrambled to his feet and glanced around.

Empty . . . except for the biggest bed he'd ever seen. And a dresser with a huge mirror, a red velvet chair, a nightstand with a frilly lamp.

A hotel?

He edged back up to the window and peeked out. Longhair guy ran into view.

Zenji stepped back.

"Man," he whispered. "Now what?"

What would his teacher-priests do in this mess? They believed that if you had compassion for people in your heart, everything would turn out well. Zenji wasn't so sure about that.

He decided they'd do one of two things: use *kendo,* their swordsmanship with bamboo sticks, or stand firm and peacefully face the problem.

Zenji didn't know kendo.

Someone in the street shouted, "He's here! I smell um."

The bedroom door flew open and slammed against the wall. A Chinese man the size of a garbage truck stood in the doorway with a baseball bat. He looked hard at Zenji and quickly took in every corner of the room.

Zenji staggered back. "It's not what you think, mister."

The big man pointed the bat at him as he came into the room, circling to his right, his eyes never leaving Zenji.

"I didn't mean to break in. . . . Some guys down on the street chased me. I was just walking to my job."

The man moved close enough to hammer Zenji's brains to mush.

Zenji put his palms out, trying to stop him. "I . . . I just got a job at the harbor, and—"

"You know what this place is?" the man snapped. "You *really* want to bus' in here? What's your name?"

Zenji looked for a way out. There wasn't one. "Zenji . . . Watanabe."

The big man studied him, then lowered the bat.

He stepped over to the window and looked out. "I don't see nobody."

"They're out there. Three of them. I didn't do anything to them."

The big man grunted. "You Japanee, that's what you did.

3

Come. You gotta get out of Chinatown. Stupid to come here."

Zenji followed him down the hall. Four young women stuck their heads out from different doors.

"Hey, Jesse, who you got there? What's going on?"

"Not'ing. Kid got the wrong address."

Oh, jeese, Zenji thought. Now he knew what this place was.

He tried to smile at the women.

Heat rushed to his face when one blew him a kiss.

Jesse took Zenji out to the street, looking right, then left. He pointed with his chin to three guys crossing toward them, ignoring a honking car.

"That's them," Zenji said.

"They jus' kids."

"Maybe, but there's three of them and one of me."

The three guys strutted around Zenji, staring him down, ignoring Jesse.

Zenji kept his mouth shut.

Be calm. Don't show fear.

"We go," Jesse said. "I take you out of here."

Zenji shook his head. "No. Thanks, but . . . I can take care of this."

Jesse stared at him. "You crazy?"

"Prob'ly."

Jesse hesitated, and stepped back.

Long-hair guy blocked the sidewalk. Barefoot, street-dirty feet, khaki pants, tight black T-shirt, a small star tattooed on his left earlobe, and eyes that darted like a lizard.

The two other guys moved in around him. Their faces said *You going get hurt, Japanee.*

Zenji tried to drag up some Buddhist compassion. These guys are just . . . these guys are . . .

Scary.

Think!

Okay. They hate me. But I don't have to hate them. Look them in the eye. Show no fear.

Long-Hair grunted. "We going take your head off today, Japanee punk. What you t'ink?"

"I'm not going to fight you."

Long-Hair leaned into Zenji's face. "Sissy, you?"

Zenji didn't blink.

Jesse crossed his arms, and people on the sidewalk watched, silent.

They're just guys like me, Zenji told himself. No different.

Long-Hair and Zenji stared into each other's eyes.

Breathe. Long, slow breath.

Think.

He's just a guy. Got a little sister.

A dog.

His mother likes him.

Maybe.

Zenji almost choked on a laugh.

Finally, Long-Hair stepped back. "Pfff. Beat it, Jap punk. Nex' time we not going be so nice."

Zenji nodded and eased around the three guys. He wanted to say something back. Friendly.

Don't push it. Could be they're just afraid of Jesse.

Zenji nodded to the big guy and walked away.

He glanced back over his shoulder.

Long-Hair ran a finger across his throat.

After he turned the corner, Zenji stopped and took deep breaths. He held his trembling hands out, palms down.

He looked again at the streets of Chinatown in surprise. He was trembling not because he was afraid, but because he'd just discovered something: that smile inside?

It was real.

Dang. Those priests were good.

2

GLASS

Zenji Watanabe was Nisei, meaning he was American-born Japanese. His parents were immigrants from Okinawa, Japan. In June he'd graduated near the top of his class from McKinley High School. Now he was driving a forklift, loading cargo onto ships while trying to figure out his next step.

Zenji daydreamed about becoming a priest—which his older brother, Henry, thought was the funniest thing he'd ever heard—but he wasn't sure what he wanted to do with his life. His Japanese school principal had encouraged him to go to Japan to study Buddhism. But that would be a long haul.

Zenji's other thoughts were to become a policeman, or maybe join the army. He'd been in JROTC, the Junior Reserve Officers' Training Corps, in high school and liked it.

"Rotsie," they called it. But Ma was adamantly against the army idea. "You forget Germany, making trouble all over. What if they make trouble with us, too? In the army, you could get killed."

Ma was too protective, like a dog shielding her puppy.

Zenji could only shake his head. Germany was on the other side of the world. How could they make trouble with the U.S.?

For now, his job at the harbor was okay.

But Zenji had a skill most guys his age did not: language. He spoke perfect English and perfect Japanese. He even understood a few words of Filipino, Chinese, and Hawaiian, picked up at work.

He lived a few miles inland in Pauoa with his mother; his fifteen-year-old sister, Aiko; and his brother, Henry, who was nineteen. Their father had been killed in an accident at his job when Zenji was eight.

Henry was an ace with numbers. Hawaiian Pineapple Company hired him right out of high school as an assistant bookkeeper, which was good. The family needed the money. Plus, he was going to the university part-time to get a degree in accounting. But Zenji knew Henry really went there to meet girls and go dancing. "One day you'll understand, little brother," Henry said. "Girls make the world go around."

Zenji laughed it off. "Girls make people nervous, you mean. What do you say to them?"

Henry tapped Zenji's chest with the back of his hand. "Don't worry. I'll teach you."

That made Zenji even more nervous.

But he knew Henry *really* wanted to join the army like

most of his friends. It was a good place to get a start in life. And besides, Pop had been in the army back in Japan. But Henry made more money at Hawaiian Pineapple.

Zenji liked the idea of signing up, too. He and Henry talked about it a lot, but not in front of Ma. "At least the army would be a job."

"More than that," Henry said. "Think of the respect you'd get."

"From who?"

"Everyone."

"Except Ma."

Henry could only nod.

Japan was making war noises these days, and their mother had heard people talking about it. Zenji noticed it at work, too. Fewer and fewer ships had brought goods in from Japan.

"I heard some guys at the harbor," Zenji said. "They say us, the British, the Chinese, and the Dutch are making it hard for Japan to get oil, so not so many ships."

Henry frowned. "Not good. With the Axis alliance and Japan siding with Germany and Italy, we could end up fighting our own relatives."

"That would be crazy."

But joining the army was impossible. The family would starve without their two paychecks. Like Henry, Zenji gave his money to Ma each month.

Ma was strict, but she had a creative side, too. She wrote poems in Kanji characters, in a style she had invented. Then she'd have Zenji or Aiko write them out in English. They were seven-line poems: one word, two words, three words, four words, three words, two words, one word. Even though

Zenji, Aiko, and Henry often made fun of them, the poems made them feel good. They held the family together.

There was one about Henry taped to the wall in the kitchen.

> *Boy*
> *Must become*
> *Man too soon,*
> *But God gave boy*
> *The strength to*
> *Be the*
> *Man.*

And for Aiko:

> *Girl*
> *On bike*
> *On busy street*
> *Must watch for people*
> *And not thoughtlessly*
> *Scare them*
> *Silly.*

Ma started writing the poems after Pop died.

Pop, a dry-dock welder at Pearl Harbor, had fallen from his scaffolding. The memory of that day was still so painful Zenji could hardly let himself think about it. But he would make Pop proud. Somehow. Even if Pop wasn't there to see it.

* * *

Zenji was eating lunch at work, sitting on a crate and looking out over the harbor. Behind him in the shade, two Hawaiian guys were joking about how cooks at Chinese restaurants were grinding glass into food served to Japanese customers.

Zenji stopped eating. "Wait a minute," he said, turning. "What's that about glass?"

The two guys stared at him.

Zenji looked down, embarrassed at his boldness. These guys were at least forty. He wasn't even half that.

But this was important. He glanced back up.

One guy winked. "Check your food, kid."

They laughed.

Ground glass was still on his mind as he walked home—not through Chinatown.

For sure, what Japan had done in Nanking was bad. But it didn't have anything to do with him. He was *American* Japanese. The closest he'd ever been to Japan was at Japanese school, where he'd learned about Japanese culture.

He kicked a crushed cigarette pack as he walked home on a road with no sidewalks. He passed small houses, where kids played in the street, moving out of the way for passing cars.

"Hey, punk!" someone called.

Zenji turned and grinned. "You the punk. How's it? What's up?"

Tosh Otani, Zenji's best friend since forever, slouched across the street. "Waiting for Naomi. You need a girlfriend, too."

"No, I don't."

Tosh shoved him playfully. "You the most chicken guy I know when it comes to girls."

"I like girls."

"Could fool me. Hey, how's the job?"

"Good. Except I almost got killed in Chinatown." He told Tosh the story. About the glass rumor, too.

"Whoa. Stay out of that place," Tosh said.

"Right."

Tosh tapped the side of Zenji's arm. "Gotta run." He pointed his chin.

Naomi was heading toward them, two blocks away.

Zenji waved to her and kept going.

Ahead, he saw a small group of people. They seemed upset.

He picked up his pace.

3
THE DOG

Zenji spotted a small black-and-white dog with a stubby tail leaning into a fence across the street. Its eyes were closed.

"What's going on?" Zenji asked a young Japanese woman who was hugging a small boy.

She hesitated. "Who are you?"

"Zenji Watanabe. I live about a half mile from here. Is that your dog?"

"My son's." The woman's eyes flooded. "We were walking. A car came and . . . Nami . . . the dog . . . went under it. I thought he'd been killed . . . but he crawled to the fence. He won't let us get close."

The sight of the shivering dog almost made Zenji sick.

Do something!

13

"I'll take a look."

The dog was struggling to breathe. At least one leg was broken. Blood trickled out of its ears, and who knew what was broken inside.

"You sure got beat up, little guy."

The dog growled when Zenji tried to touch it.

Zenji stood and went back to the woman and the boy. "I can help you get your dog to your house."

The boy broke free and ran off.

Zenji watched as he raced down the street. It was exactly what he'd done when Ma told him Pop had died.

"Thank you," the woman said, "but his father . . ."

Zenji knew how it went. You put a badly injured dog out of its misery. You didn't let it suffer. Who had money to fix a pet?

"I understand," he said, and thought for a moment. "Look, I'll take the dog to my house. Maybe I can help him. If I can, where do you live so I can bring him back?"

Even as he said it he had doubts. How do you fix a broken dog? But Aiko would help him. And Ma.

The woman pointed. "The green house."

Zenji nodded. "What's your son's name?"

"Ken. The dog is Nami. Thank you, Zenji Watanabe. I need to go to my son."

She hurried off, and Zenji found a fruit crate in the weeds.

He took off his shirt, wrapped it around Nami, and gently lifted him into the crate.

This time, not one yip.

"Let's get out of here, boy."

When he turned down his quiet street the first thing he saw was a car. A rare sight—nobody in his neighborhood had a car.

It was parked in front of his house.

BRIGHT STAR IN PARADISE

Zenji took the crate to the back of the house, trying to peek in the window to see who was there. But the sun glared on the glass.

There was a small toolshed under the banyan tree. It was cool and dark inside. The only light came from a small window.

Zenji set the crate on the dirt floor and squatted next to it. "I'll be back, Nami. Don't you die on me, you hear?"

He ran to the house, crept up the back steps, inched the screen door open, and tiptoed through the kitchen.

His mother was saying "I'm sorry. I don't understand" in Japanese.

"I'm here to see Zenji, Mrs. Watanabe," a man said in English. His voice was familiar. "I'm sorry. You don't understand me, do you?"

Zenji's jaw dropped when he stepped into the room. "Colonel Blake!"

Ma turned, startled. *"Shizuka dattakara!"* You were so quiet!

"Sorry, Ma," Zenji said in Japanese. "Where's Aiko?"

"Ieni wa inaiyo." Not home.

Colonel Blake stood and broke into a huge grin. "It's good to see you, Zenji."

He reached out his hand.

Zenji shook. "What the heck are you doing here, Colonel?"

Colonel Blake laughed. "Something's come up, and you're the first person I thought of."

Ma whispered to Zenji, "Who is this man? What does he want?"

"He's my old commanding officer in JROTC. Remember the army thing Henry and I did in high school? I don't know what he wants."

Ma sat back, stiff. To have a haole, a white person, in her house was a grave matter. A visit from the president would not have been more shocking.

Colonel Blake looked at Zenji. "Does your mother understand English?"

"Not much."

Colonel Blake bowed slightly toward Ma. "Please thank her for her hospitality."

Zenji did.

Ma nodded, almost imperceptibly.

"Please, Colonel. Sit."

"What does he want?" Ma whispered again.

"I'm trying to find out." Zenji turned back to the colonel. "She wants to know why you're here."

17

"It concerns . . . a job."

"I have a job, sir."

Zenji found himself right back in JROTC, calling Colonel Blake *sir*.

"This job is more important."

Must be, Zenji thought. Why would the colonel come all the way up here to talk to me?

Ma tugged on Zenji's sleeve.

"He wants to talk about a job, Ma."

Ma's face brightened. "He's not asking you to join the army? That's no place for you."

"What's wrong with the army?"

"In the army you die."

"Ma, it's okay. He just wants to talk."

Ma pushed herself up off the couch. Zenji and the colonel stood as Ma bowed and went into the kitchen.

"Is there a problem?" the colonel asked.

"Naw, it's just her way. She's very protective."

"As she should be."

"What's this about, Colonel?"

"As I remember, you were excellent with languages."

Zenji looked down. He wasn't used to compliments. "Only Japanese and English. Couple words in Chinese, and some Hawaiian. Filipino, too. I mean, what they call Tagalog."

Colonel Blake smiled. "You like to travel, Zenji?"

"Never been off the island. But I've sure thought about it."

"Zenji, I want you to do something for me."

"Name it, sir."

"You know where Central Intermediate School is?"

"Sure."

"Can you be there tomorrow morning at nine o'clock sharp?"

"Well . . . I'd like to, but I have to work."

"It's all set. I called your boss."

"You know where I work?" Zenji stared at him. How did he know that? "And Mr. Santos said it was okay?"

"I told him it was important."

Zenji started to ask why but stopped. His family and the priests at Japanese school had taught him: respect authority. Never question it.

Nami! He'd almost forgotten. The dog needed help.

"Zenji?"

"Uh, yes, sir. I'll be there."

"I knew I could count on you."

Zenji followed the colonel to the door. "Keep this little conversation under your hat," the colonel said. "You can tell your family, but that's it, okay?"

"Yes, sir . . . but why?"

Colonel Blake looked down. "Can't say right now. But there's no doubt in my mind that you're the man they need."

"Need for what?"

"You'll see."

They went down the steps. The birds had stopped yakking in the trees, and the sky was painted the soft blue-gray of evening.

Colonel Blake looked up, and Zenji followed his gaze. One bright star had appeared.

"Venus," Colonel Blake said. "Another night in paradise."

Zenji nodded, though it was just his dirt street and the end of another hot day.

Colonel Blake tapped Zenji's arm. "Nine o'clock sharp."

"Got it, sir."

As Colonel Blake drove off, Zenji ran around the house to Nami.

5

SUSPICION

Aiko skidded to a stop next to the shed, the rear tire of her bike fanning out dirt.

"Jeese, Aiko! You want to give me a heart attack?"

"You have a heart?"

"Funny."

Aiko was as tough as any boy her age, and the boys knew it. Zenji called her the Watanabe Warrior, which she loved.

"Come," Zenji said. "I want to show you something."

Inside, they knelt over the crate. "A puppy?" she said. "It looks sick."

"He was hit by a car, and he's not mine."

"Whose is it?"

"Kid named Ken. His mother didn't know what to do. I said I'd help."

Aiko leaned in. "You poor thing."

"His name is Nami."

"Nami," Aiko whispered. She bent close to look at the dog's broken leg. "We have to fix that."

"Yeah, but how?"

Aiko chewed on her lip. "Find some short straight sticks. I'll get something to wrap around the leg, and some string. We're going to put him back together."

Aiko ran to the house. Zenji found a board and sliced off two splints with a machete, then chopped them down to size.

Ma came back with Aiko. "What's this?"

Zenji looked over his shoulder. "A car hit him, Ma."

"Let me see."

Zenji moved aside.

Gently, Ma felt Nami's ribs, legs, and neck. "Get a bowl of water and a rag. This dog needs to drink."

Zenji hurried back to the house. He'd known Ma and Aiko would want to help Nami!

When he got back, Nami's leg was bound tight to the splints with cloth and string. Ma soaked the rag in the water and let the dog suck on it. "What we just did to his leg must have been painful. Yet he was silent." She stroked his head. "You're a brave dog."

"Will he be okay, Ma?"

"I think so . . . if he's still alive tomorrow."

When Henry came home Zenji took him to the shed. Nami was sleeping. "Always wanted a dog," Henry said. "Too bad he got hurt."

"Ma said he might make it."

"She would know."

Ma's parents had a little farm in Japan. They were poor, but they took good care of their animals. She'd been sixteen when she married Pop and came to the islands looking for better work.

Henry stroked Nami. "Aiko said some haole stopped by today."

"Colonel Blake."

"From JROTC?"

"Yep."

"Good guy," Henry said. "I almost went into the army because of him."

Zenji squatted down next to Nami. "He came in the house."

"Ma let him in?"

"What could she do?"

"Wow. First time a haole set foot in our house. . . . Was she nervous?"

Zenji shook his head. "Suspicious."

Henry whistled, low. "The neighbors will talk."

"Let um."

"Yeah, who cares?"

"He wants to talk to me about a job."

"In the army?"

"He said he couldn't tell me."

"Is that so."

Zenji stood. "I'm supposed to show up at Central Intermediate School tomorrow morning."

"Why?"

"You tell me. What do you think he wants?"

Henry shrugged. "Maybe he wants to invite you up to Schofield with Nick and Takeo, make you a soldier."

Henry's two high school friends had joined up right after graduation. Now they were at boot camp. There was a war going on in Europe, but the U.S. was at peace, so they'd be safe.

Zenji scoffed. "I'm too young."

"I guess this time tomorrow we can talk about it, huh?"

That night, Zenji slept on the dirt floor of the shed.

He kept getting up to check on Nami and give him water. He couldn't sleep anyway. Everything was too weird. Chinese guys wanting to beat him up and put glass in his food. A broken dog. Colonel Blake.

He finally dozed off just before dawn.

When he woke, sunlight was streaming through the window. He popped up, squinting.

Ma was kneeling by the crate. "You were snoring. You must have been awake all night."

"Pretty much. How is he?"

"Look."

The dog blinked and lifted his head.

Zenji grinned.

Ma soaked the rag and squeezed water into Nami's mouth. "You late for work already. Get up. I'll make you rice and egg."

"What time is it, Ma? I got to be at the school."

Ma said nothing.

"Ma, it's just about a job, and it could pay more. That would be good, right?"

"We don't need more. We're fine."

Nami gave a whispery woof.

Zenji stroked his head. "That's what I say, too."

He hurried to the house, wondering what he would find at the school. Maybe Ma was right to be nervous.

Nah. Colonel Blake would never steer him wrong.

6
SIX MEN

When Zenji arrived at the school Colonel Blake wasn't anywhere in sight, so Zenji entered alone. A uniformed man stood when he walked in.

"Good morning. Follow me."

He led Zenji to a room where six uniformed men—two army and four navy—sat behind a long table.

Zenji gawked.

An army guy stood, name plate HACKNER. "Zenji Watanabe?"

"Yes, sir."

"Thank you for coming." He motioned toward a metal chair facing the men. "Please sit."

This was an interview? It felt more like he'd been arrested and was about to be grilled. What had Colonel Blake gotten him into? Where was he, anyway?

"We're here from Washington, D.C.," Hackner began, motioning to the men at the table. "We're conducting interviews with special candidates such as yourself. May we begin?"

Candidates? Washington, D.C.?

"Y-yes, sir."

There was a long moment of silence as Hackner looked over some papers. The five other men stared at Zenji. Each had a glass of water, a pen, and a notepad in front of him.

"Mr. Watanabe, your former JROTC commanding officer, Colonel Blake, gives you a very high recommendation."

Ho! Hackner had spoken in Japanese! *Perfect* Japanese. Zenji had never heard a haole speak Japanese like that. His inflections and mannerisms were flawless.

"Mr. Watanabe?"

"Uh, thank you, sir."

"You may speak in Japanese."

"Yes," Zenji said, switching to Japanese. "Thank you, sir."

Did they *all* speak Japanese?

Hackner went on. "Where were you born?"

"Honolulu."

"Were your parents born here?"

"No, sir, they were born in Okinawa, Japan."

"So they're still citizens of Japan?"

"Yes, sir."

The officers scribbled notes. They *did* speak Japanese.

"When did your parents arrive in the islands?"

Zenji thought. "Around 1920, I guess. I don't know for sure."

"What work does your father do?"

"He was killed when I was eight years old. He was a welder at Pearl Harbor."

"I see. I'm sorry."

"Thank you, sir."

"You wear glasses. What's your vision like without them?"

What a weird question. "Okay for long distances. Close up it's fuzzy, but not bad."

Hackner nodded.

"Have you ever been to Japan?"

"No, sir."

"Do you have a desire to go to Japan?"

"Maybe someday, sure."

All six men wrote something on their pads.

"Would you relocate there?"

"No, sir. I like it here. This is my home."

"Any other place you'd like to visit?"

Zenji considered that for a moment. "Los Angeles. I've always wanted to go to the mainland."

"Why?"

"Just heard about it."

"Do you have a girlfriend?"

Zenji blinked. "No, sir."

Who's your best friend?"

"A guy named Tosh Otani. I've known him all my life."

"What does he do?"

"Works with his dad."

"What kind of work?"

"Yard work . . . for rich people."

For the next six hours, even while they ate the box lunches that an aide brought in, Zenji answered questions. Some seemed pointless, like whom he hung out with in high school. But he answered as if each one was important.

Where was all this going?

The final question confused him even more. "Can you make yourself available for the next three days?"

"I have a job . . . but . . . maybe I can work it out."

"Good. Be here again at oh-nine-hundred tomorrow. We have some tests for you to take with the other candidates."

"Other candidates?"

"Twenty-nine more." Hackner smiled, his first of the day.

All his life Zenji had been told: never question authority. Even so, he usually had a million things to ask.

Today, when he walked back out into the sun, he had only one: what the spit was going on?

IN THE ARMY YOU DIE

"**S**o tell us," Henry said at dinner as they ate Ma's cabbage soup. "What happened at the school?"

Zenji looked at Ma, who acted as if she hadn't heard.

"Well . . . it was an interview."

"About what?"

"Where I went to school, who my friends are, where Ma and Pop came from, had I ever been to Japan, did I want to go there."

Henry slapped his leg. "I knew it!"

"Knew what?"

"I've been hearing rumors that the army and the FBI have been keeping track of Japanese."

Ma stopped eating and looked at him. "Why?"

"Politics."

"What politics?" Zenji said. "And why are they talking to me, not you?"

Henry drummed his fingers on the table. "I don't get that part, either."

"Don't talk to the army, either of you," Ma said. "You already have work."

Henry pointed his soupspoon at Zenji. "I think this is about more than a job, Ma."

Ma scowled. "No army!"

"It's okay, Ma," Henry said.

She looked away, grim.

Aiko kept quiet, but glanced at each of them.

"Get this," Zenji went on. "They all spoke Japanese! Six haole army and navy officers, all speaking perfect Japanese. Crazy."

Aiko leaned closer.

Ma's face was frozen. Zenji could barely look at her.

She laid her spoon on the table. "You are *not* joining the army. I don't care what they say or what they pay. No army! In the army you die."

"Ma, you don't die in the army."

"Your father died."

"He worked for the *navy*, Ma, not the army, and the navy didn't kill him. It was an accident."

"Same-same."

Zenji sighed. "Ma . . . listen . . . even if I was in the army, there's no war. How could I die? And anyway, they're talking to a bunch of other guys, too, not just me."

"There were more guys?" Henry said.

"They called us candidates."

"For what?"

"That's the big question."

Henry squinted. "Be careful, Zenji."

"Why?"

"For one, why do you think the army is interested in the fact that you speak Japanese?"

Zenji waited. He had no idea.

"Think about it. You've heard the rumors. We have deteriorating relations with Japan. And Japan and Germany are allies. And Germany is making war. Two plus two equals four, little brother, and it all sounds like trouble to me."

Ma snapped, "Whatever those men want, you say no!"

For the next three days, Zenji and twenty-nine other young Japanese guys took exams and translated from English to Japanese and Japanese to English—conversations, instructions, radio news reports.

Why, why, why?

Meanwhile, Nami slept in the crate, now padded with rags. Ma doted on him. There was even a new poem taped to the kitchen wall.

> *Small*
> *Dog in*
> *Box is like*
> *Weeds in back yard.*
> *Strong will to*
> *Live long*
> *Life.*

Zenji liked that one better than the one he found on the wall in the room he shared with Henry:

> *Messy*
> *Room like*
> *This must mean*
> *Mongoose came in house*
> *Thinking this place*
> *Is garbage*
> *Can.*

He laughed, then started cleaning up.

Later, he stopped by Ken's house and told Ken's mother that Nami was getting better every day. "Come see him."

A few days later, Zenji went out to the shed, where Ma sat with Nami. "He's looking good, Ma. You're a miracle maker."

"He did it himself. This morning Ken came by, and Nami tried to stand."

"That's good, Ma. Thank you for taking care of him."

She waved her hand. "It's nothing."

"No. It's everything."

One day a couple of weeks later, Ma and Aiko were sitting on the porch steps when Zenji got home from work. Ma handed him a note.

"That army man brought it."

Ma waited, eyes pinned on Zenji. Aiko stood and leaned against him as he opened it.

*Outstanding news, Zenji! You made it! The
board unanimously chose you first, over all the
other candidates. I dropped by to congratulate you.
I'll be back on Saturday around noon to fill you in.
See you then.*

Colonel Blake

Zenji looked up. He could have a job that paid good
money! Maybe in Los Angeles! He smiled, wanting to run
over to Tosh's house and tell him.

But Zenji knew better than to celebrate in front of Ma.
"Colonel Blake is coming here on Saturday, Ma . . . maybe
about a job, and . . . maybe on the mainland."

Aiko clutched his arm.

"What about becoming a priest?" Ma said.

"That was just an idea I had, Ma. This could be good. I
could get better pay and I've never been to the mainland."

Zenji couldn't look her in the eye. The world seemed much
larger now. He wanted to do everything she didn't want him
to do, like go see Los Angeles.

Ma's eyes narrowed. She pushed herself up and went into
the house.

Aiko stared at him. "I don't want you going anywhere,
either!"

8

BE BOLD

On Saturday, Zenji was sitting on the front steps waiting for Colonel Blake, practicing a trick: rolling a coin over his knuckles from one side of his hand to the other. He was starting to get the hang of it when the colonel's car pulled up.

The colonel waved as Zenji headed to the car. "Let's go for a ride."

"Where are we going?"

"Fort Shafter."

Zenji got in. Ho, if Ma knew about this she'd faint!

The warm day smelled good, like ripe mangoes, with a hint of mint and ocean air. Questions cooked inside Zenji's head, but he figured the colonel wanted to surprise him, so he kept quiet.

Patience.

Like the Buddhist priests.

Fort Shafter was like nothing Zenji had ever seen. Men hustled around in uniform, big lawns and old monkeypod trees surrounded white buildings. Bougainvillea sprouted in reds and oranges.

They parked and walked toward a building: *Headquarters, Hawaiian Department, United States Army.*

Colonel Blake smiled. "Nervous?"

"Should I be?"

The colonel slapped Zenji on the back. "Not you. You're made of something special."

Inside, they entered a door marked G2. ARMY INTELLI-GENCE. COLONEL SUTHERLAND.

Colonel Sutherland stood behind a metal desk. An American flag and framed certificates decorated the wall behind him. He grinned as he walked around to shake hands with Colonel Blake. "Thank you for bringing this lad down here." Colonel Sutherland shook with Zenji. "So you were top dog in the competition, you know that? It's good to meet you."

Zenji blinked. "Thank you, sir."

Colonel Sutherland motioned them toward a couch. He pulled his desk chair around and sat leaning forward.

"That test was especially difficult. We want the best of the best, and we found two. You're one. Congratulations."

Zenji was almost dizzy. What was he getting into?

"Colonel Blake tells me you excelled in ROTC."

"JROTC, sir. It was a good program."

"Have you ever thought of making a career in the military?"

He wanted to say: With *my* mother? "I liked Rotsie, sir. My brother did, too."

"What do you think about traveling away from the islands?"

"I'd love to see Los Angeles, sir."

"We want to offer you a job, Zenji, an important one that involves travel. Sound interesting?"

"Yes, sir, it does." But it sure won't to Ma.

"Great! But not Los Angeles. Manila."

"The Philippines?"

"Too far away?"

"No, sir, I just thought . . . well, the mainland, the U.S."

"The Philippines are a U.S. commonwealth."

"Right."

"We urgently need a man with your skills in Manila working for intelligence as a translator. Your talent is important to this country. I have to ask you to keep this conversation under your hat, all right?"

"Yes, sir."

Wow, Zenji thought. *Important to this country?*

Henry's words echoed in his head. *Be careful.*

"But . . . my mother, sir . . . she won't like it."

"That may be true, but this is absolutely critical. The army *needs* you, Zenji."

The army.

There it was.

But.

"So, I would just translate Japanese to English? That kind of work?"

"To start, yes."

"There's more?"

"There's always more."

Zenji nodded. "How long would I be in Manila?"

"Hard to say, but at least a year."

"When would I leave?"

"Soon. Weeks at most."

Colonel Blake smiled. "Shall we sign you up?"

"Now?"

"Why not?"

Be bold, Zenji thought. Do you want to spend your life moving pallets at the wharf? Ma would get over it. Still . . .

"My family needs me to help out. My father died when I was eight."

"You can send every penny of your pay home."

Zenji felt an excitement inside, like a wave building. He was out of school now, a man, and he should make his own decisions.

But there was a knot in his gut. Ma might stop speaking to him.

But she would come around.

He hoped.

"Colonel Blake, I think it might be appropriate for you to do the honors," Colonel Sutherland said.

Zenji stood when the men stood.

"Sir . . . don't you need to be eighteen to join the army?"

"You're not eighteen?"

"Seventeen . . . sir."

"Ah. Then we need your mother's consent. I'm sure she'll be proud to hear that you did so well."

They had no idea.

"Yes, sir." Zenji's head was spinning.

Colonel Blake continued. "Zenji Watanabe, raise your right hand and repeat after me. I do solemnly swear . . ."

"I, Zenji Watanabe, do solemnly swear . . ."

"That I will support and defend the Constitution of the United States against all enemies, foreign and domestic; that I will bear true faith and allegiance to the same; and that I will obey the orders of the president of the United States and orders of the officers appointed over me, according to the regulations and the Uniform Code of Military Justice. So help me God."

Zenji Watanabe was in the United States Army.

9
THE MARK

As they drove away from the base Zenji said, "It's weird, sir. Already I feel different. Excited, and nervous . . . and . . . well, everything happened so fast. I'm kind of stunned. Am I *really* in the army?"

"Buck private, CIP. That's the Corps of Intelligence Police."

"Police?"

"More intelligence than police."

Zenji could almost hear the wheels spinning inside his head. "Intelligence—isn't that spying?"

"It's a lot of things regarding information, Zenji."

That made sense. But the word *spy* wouldn't go away.

"Hey, there's a little place ahead we could stop for a soda," Colonel Blake said. "Would you like that?"

"Sure."

"I've got something I want to share with you."

They sat at a picnic table with ice-cold Cokes. The colonel rotated the bottle in his hands, not drinking.

"Zenji," the colonel started, "you know a few things about me: U.S. Army officer, ROTC, married, one son."

Zenji nodded.

"My wife, Shirley, was born and raised here."

He was silent a moment. Then he went on. "Our son, John, wanted to be a military man, too . . . but he eloped with a girl in college. Now he's a fireman in Virginia." Colonel Blake smiled. "He was nervous about telling us he'd gotten married. We all do some crazy things when we're young."

"Yes, sir," Zenji said.

Crazy . . . like joining the army.

The colonel paused. "You know, you've always reminded me of John. He has the same quiet determination that you do. You're a lot alike. Strong."

Why is he telling me this? The colonel had always been pretty formal.

Zenji's mind flooded with memories of his own father—his mechanic's fingernail grime, his battered old lunch box, his work boots on the porch, the way he brought the smell of oil and sweat into the house with him.

"I know this is . . . unexpected." Zenji startled as the colonel went on. "But today I couldn't be more proud of you. Wherever you go, whatever you do, Shirley and I will be with you. I just want you to know that."

Zenji looked up. "I don't know what to say, sir . . . except that . . . well, I feel honored."

Colonel Blake smiled.

They sat in silence as the colonel finished his Coke. "Let's go see your mother. Something tells me this may not go easy."

"No, sir. She's going to fall on the floor."

The buzz of the city faded as they drove into Zenji's quiet neighborhood. As they parked, Aiko and her friends looked up from playing with Nami, who was now well enough to limp around out of the box.

Zenji took a deep breath as they walked up to the front door. "Ma? Colonel Blake is with me." They went inside.

Ma came out from the kitchen, got down on her hands and knees, and bowed her head nearly to the floor.

"Please, tell her to stand up."

"It's Japanese, Colonel."

Zenji pointed toward a chair.

The colonel sat.

"Ma," Zenji said, helping her to her feet, "Colonel Blake wants to talk with you about something important."

Ma wouldn't look at Zenji.

"Tell him I will be right back with tea," she said.

"It's all right, Ma. He only has a minute."

She hesitated, and sat on the couch with her hands folded in her lap.

"Mrs. Watanabe," the colonel began. He paused, and Zenji saw deep sympathy in his eyes. Zenji's heart began to race.

Colonel Blake spoke gently. "Your son has recently participated in a very difficult competition. His language skills were tested over and over. Among thirty applicants, all college graduates, Zenji was number one. No one else performed at his level. It was truly impressive."

The colonel waited for Zenji to translate.

Ma listened, her face impossible to read.

Zenji nodded for the colonel to go on.

"The government is in critical need of the very skills Zenji has, and we have an extremely important job for him. This job does not involve weapons, Mrs. Watanabe. He will be safe."

Zenji translated.

Ma studied her hands.

The colonel leaned forward. "Since Zenji is underage, we would like your consent for him to join the United States Army. We *seriously* need his help. I wouldn't be here if we didn't."

Ma listened to Zenji translate, motionless. Zenji could hardly look at her, each word felt dark and heavy. There was no easy way to say them.

A scratching at the door caused him to look up. Nami was standing on his hind legs with his front paws on the screen, Aiko beside him, hands cupped around her eyes, peering in.

"If it's all right with you, Mrs. Watanabe," Colonel Blake went on, hesitantly extending the papers, "would you please just sign here." He pulled out a pen.

Ma looked at the pen and papers, but didn't reach for them.

Zenji knew that even though she was torn, she would agree. Colonel Blake was authority and he was haole. She would sign.

Colonel Blake turned to Zenji.

"She can't write English, sir. Only Kanji."

"She can sign in Kanji, then, and I can verify it with my signature."

Zenji took the papers and knelt before his mother. Neither could look the other in the eye.

"Ma, he wants you to sign your name. And, Ma? I want to do this. It's a good job and I can send you all my pay. It's a chance for me to—"

Ma took the papers. "Where?"

Zenji peeked up at her. "Right here, Ma," he said softly.

What strength it took for her to take the pen from his hand. She signed her name.

Zenji handed the papers to the colonel, who signed. "Thank you, Mrs. Watanabe," he said, so quietly that Zenji could barely hear him. "Thank you."

Zenji held his breath.

The colonel stood, bowed, and went to the door. Zenji followed, leaving his mother dazed on the couch.

Aiko grabbed Nami and ran around to the backyard.

Out on the street the colonel looked at the house. "I know it took immense courage for your mother to do what she just did."

"You do?"

"I would not have asked you—or her—to do this if it wasn't absolutely vital."

"What exactly will I be doing?"

Colonel Blake held up his hand. "I don't know enough to tell you, Zenji. Truly."

Zenji jumped when Aiko flew out from the backyard on

her bike and raced down the street. What's with her? he thought.

Colonel Blake came to attention and saluted. "Carry on, Buck Private."

Zenji saluted back.

As the colonel drove away, Zenji turned to look at his house. How could he go back in and face Ma?

He sighed and walked up the old road to where the houses ended and the jungle began. It took him an hour to walk back, and still he couldn't go inside.

10
MACHETES

"**Y**ou're in?"

Henry shook Zenji awake. He'd been working late.

Zenji sat up. "What time is it?"

"Past my bedtime. Ma's still up. She was just sitting in the kitchen with only a candle for light. Had to pry the news out of her."

"Yeah, I'm in. Buck private."

Henry raised his eyebrows. "You got Ma to sign? You're not old enough."

"Why did you say be careful about the army?"

"They can be persuasive." Henry spat in his hand. "Shake, brother. At least one of us can see the world."

Zenji grinned and spat in his own. "I'm going to Manila."

"Machetes."

"Headhunters."

"Cannibals. Kill you in the night."

They laughed; that was what Ma said about Filipinos. Rumors like that ran rampant around Honolulu. Everybody loved a spooky story.

"You tell Tosh yet?"

Zenji shook his head.

"How come?"

"I didn't want to leave Ma. You weren't home yet."

"When are you leaving?"

Zenji shrugged. "Soon."

"What about boot camp?"

"Nobody said."

Henry nodded. "Very mysterious. Anyway, tell Tosh. We can have a shipping-out party."

"I'm supposed to keep quiet about it."

"Don't worry. It would just be us guys . . . maybe some girls."

Zenji grinned. Henry never gave up.

"I bet we could get you a date."

"No," Zenji said. He was tempted, but that was all he needed, a girl to make his life even more confusing.

"Stick with me and Tosh, little brother. We know what we're doing."

"That's what worries me."

A few days later, Zenji sat in shorts and T-shirt on the back porch watching Aiko chase Nami around the yard. The dog's limp was just about gone. He'd been with them almost a month now.

"Time to take him back to Ken," Zenji said.

Aiko looked up.

"He's better, Aiko."

"Not fair," she said. "He goes, then you go."

"I'll write you."

"It's not the same."

"Yeah. I know."

Aiko came to sit beside him, their shoulders touching. Zenji crossed his arms over his knees. The house behind him felt like a ten-ton boulder on his back.

Ma was not speaking to him.

And now he'd quit his job at the harbor. Zenji had told Mr. Santos he'd joined the army and would be shipping out soon.

Mr. Santos had slapped Zenji's back. "Buck private, huh? You gotta start somewhere. You'll do well, Zenji. I'm impressed."

But Ma wasn't. Ignoring Zenji, she complained to Henry and Aiko at dinner. "Don't waste food. We have to live with less now."

"Ma, I'm going to send you all my pay. I promise."

Ma wouldn't look at him.

There was even a new poem on the kitchen wall. Zenji and Henry had read it together.

> *Rice*
> *Does not*
> *Fall from sky*
> *Like rain. Be thankful*
> *And eat with*
> *Hearts of*
> *Gratitude.*

Henry tapped it with a finger. "You know she's not upset about the money. She's upset about you going." He sighed. "It's hard for her to let go, Zenji. Even of a lazybones like you."

Zenji stared at Ma's poem.

"Here's some advice Nick picked up at Schofield: in the army, never volunteer for anything. It could get you killed."

"Don't the officers just volunteer you?"

"Well, there is that."

Now, Nami whined, his tail wagging as he looked at Zenji and Aiko.

"Come here, little warrior." Zenji set Nami on the step beside him. "I'm going to miss this place, Aiko."

"Then don't go."

"I have to."

Zenji lifted Nami into his lap. "When did the world go so crazy, little buddy? You and me, we were just minding our own business, huh?" Nami licked his hand. He wondered who the other recruit was, the one he'd be going to Manila with. He cringed, remembering Ma's reaction when he'd told her he would be leaving for the Philippines.

She'd fallen into a chair. "You're different from them, Zenji-*kun*," she pleaded. "They will cut you. They will attack you in the night."

"No, Ma, no. Where do you get such ideas?"

"Tell that colonel to send you somewhere else."

Zenji had to convince her that it was impossible to change anything. He'd be just fine. "All I'm going to do is read things and listen to the radio. Filipinos are good people just like us, Ma."

She had looked at him, gotten up, and gone outside to work in her garden, clumps of dirt flying.

Zenji had watched from the window.
He hadn't gotten a word out of her since.

After a week of listening to Japanese radio at the Federal
Building, hearing only music and meaningless chatter, Zenji
went to the library to study up on the Philippines—Manila
was the capital and was more than five thousand miles from
Honolulu; the United States got the Philippines from Spain
in 1898 after the Spanish-American War.

And Ma was right. There were cannibals and headhunters
in the deep jungles.

What? He checked the book's publication date: 1916.
Things must have changed since then.

He checked the map and found that Manila was only nine
hundred miles from Okinawa. Ma would like that. And he
would tell her that the Philippines were called the "Pearl of
the Orient." That sounded good, too.

Still, her words stuck: *They will cut you. They will attack
you in the night.*

He shut the book.

What have I done?

MINA

Three days before he was to ship out, Zenji knocked on Ken's door. When his mother answered, she beamed and reached out to Nami, who scooted close and licked her hand.

"Ken!" she called. *"Ken!"*

She hugged Zenji hard, catching him by surprise.

Ken pushed around his mother. "Nami! Nami!"

The dog leaped up, licking his face, whining.

Zenji felt a happy sadness. "Good as new. Got a little limp, is all."

Ken looked up, his smile wide.

His mother bowed. "You are welcome at our house, always."

Zenji nodded. "Thank you."

When Zenji headed to the street, Nami followed. Zenji

picked him up and carried him back to Ken. "This is your house, little warrior. But you will always be with me, I promise."

Zenji walked away, head down, kicking pebbles, his mind swirling with questions.

Little warrior.

Was joining the army the right thing to do? Was it worth hurting Ma? Making her worry? Making her stop talking to him? Would the army help him figure out what to do with his life? Or should he have become a Buddhist priest?

He snorted. He'd never make it as a priest. He could probably think like them; but he sure couldn't live like they did, so simply.

He needed more . . . excitement.

And that's what he got when Henry came home that night. "Listen up, Buck Private. Tomorrow night, me and Tosh are throwing you a shipping-out party . . . and we got you a date!"

Her name was Mina.

She was barely seventeen, and Zenji had known her all his life.

Sort of.

Their fathers had worked together at Pearl Harbor, and though they'd rarely seen each other outside of work, Mina's family had come to Pop's funeral. Zenji remembered how grateful Ma had been for their thoughtfulness.

Mina was a year behind, a senior at McKinley High.

She looked different than she had in school. Grown up. High heels, a red dress.

The first thing Zenji noticed were her eyes, shining, almost sparkling. And her lips. Red, like her dress. And her perfume.

Zenji, Henry, and Henry's new girlfriend, Lois, had just arrived at Tosh's party of eight couples, all Japanese. Zenji's friends didn't mix much with other races. Big-band music filled the front room, cleared out so people could dance. Tosh's parents had retreated to a back room for the evening.

"You remember Mina from school, right?" Tosh said.

Zenji nodded.

Mina smiled and reached out her hand. "Nice to see you again, Zenji."

Her hand was warm and silky soft, but her grip was strong. "Yeah," he said. "It's been a while."

Heat brushed across his face. Set-up dates were weird, but at least he knew her.

"You like to dance, Zenji?" Mina said, still smiling . . . as if no one else was standing there with them. "Swing?"

"Well, uh . . . I never, you know, tried it."

"Oh my," she said. "I can see I have some work to do."

No! He was *not* dancing!

Mina grabbed his hand. "Come. I'll show you."

"But—"

Tosh put his hands to his face in fake horror.

Zenji stumbled around, following Mina's patient lead. His clumsiness didn't seem to bother her at all. The dance grew wild and fast. And fun. He actually caught on.

"Well, look at you," Mina said. "You're a natural dancer!"

"You think so?"

"I *know* so."

Henry winked and Tosh cracked up, but Zenji didn't care. He was having more fun than he'd had in months.

After a while, he and Mina went outside to cool off. The night was warm, with stars like diamonds tossed across the sky.

"Thank you for being a good sport," Mina said. "Some guys won't even *try* dancing."

"A few days ago that would have been me."

"So what changed?"

He shrugged. "Well, for one, you're kind of hard to say no to."

Mina laughed. "You're funny."

"And you've grown up. You used to just be . . . a kid."

"It happens."

Zenji grinned.

"Naomi told me you joined the army."

"That's supposed to be a secret."

"Why?"

"They told me not to talk about it."

He wanted to tell her about the Pearl of the Orient and ask her if she thought there were still people around who ate other people, and what she thought about Filipinos and machetes.

Instead, he turned toward the house and the sounds of Tosh's party. "I really like that music."

"Benny Goodman."

"He's good."

"My favorite."

"Want to go back in?"

"Not unless we have to."

"No, we don't . . . have to."

She gave him a gentle push. "How come we never got to know each other?"

He grinned. "I was too . . . handsome?"

That made her laugh, loud and friendly. "Well, even though you were too good-looking, I liked you anyway."

"You did?"

"Remember . . . your dad's funeral?"

Zenji looked down. "You were there."

"You came up to my father and shook his hand," she said.

"He made Ma feel better, just by being there."

"My father talked about you for days, saying you were an eight-year-old who acted like a grown man. An old soul, he said, and very strong."

Zenji smiled. "So what about you? After high school, what?"

"I'm going to be a nurse."

He nodded. "You'll be a good one."

Surprising Zenji, Mina hooked her arm in his. "Thank you, Zenji Watanabe."

"Yeah, sure."

They were silent for a while, standing together in the yard. Zenji wondered where his nervousness about girls had gone. He felt as if he and Mina had been friends for a long time.

So strange.

"It's too bad," Mina said.

"What is?"

"You, going away. I mean, after seeing you around all my life, I'm finally just getting to know you. And more important, who am I going to dance with?"

Zenji laughed. "Lots of guys."

She was quiet for a moment. A light breeze rustled the trees in Tosh's yard. Mina gave his arm a squeeze.

"Can I write to you?"

His heart jumped. "Yes! I mean . . . sure."

THE NEXT BLUE MOON

The next night, the evening before Zenji was to ship out, he poked his head out of the kitchen when he heard Ma talking to someone at the front door. "I know you," she said. "The Tamashiro girl. Your daddy worked with my husband."

Wow, Zenji thought, smiling.

Mina bowed, holding a mango pie, fresh out of the oven. "It's good to see you again, Mrs. Watanabe."

Ma held the door open. "Please, come inside."

Mina kicked off her wooden sandals and left them on the porch as Aiko appeared next to Zenji.

Mina beamed at them. "I can't stay long, but I thought you'd all like something sweet to honor Zenji's departure."

Aiko turned to Zenji. "Your girlfriend?" she whispered.

Zenji shook his head, but he was still smiling. No girl had ever paid this kind of attention to him.

Mina held out the pie as he crossed the room. "I hope you like mango."

Zenji took it. "I love mango . . . but you didn't have to—"

"I wanted to."

"Thank her, you idiot," Aiko said.

Zenji laughed, and bowed ceremoniously. "Thank you! Mina, this is my sister, Aiko."

"Hello, Aiko."

"Zenji didn't tell me he had a girlf—"

"Mina," Zenji said, stepping in front of Aiko. "Please. Have some pie!"

"No, I can't stay. I just wanted to say . . . not goodbye, but I hope you come back soon . . . from . . ."

Zenji looked down. "I'm not supposed to say where."

She nodded.

He put down the pie and stepped outside with Mina.

"Well," Mina said, slipping on her sandals, "I like your sister. She watches out for you."

"She's a good kid."

Mina leaned in and boldly kissed Zenji on the cheek. "Remember me."

She was gone before he could recover.

"Whoa!" Aiko said. "Your first girlfriend!"

"She's not my . . . She was at Tosh's party. She's nice, isn't she?"

"That pie looks good," Aiko said. "Can I have some?"

"You stay home," Ma said. "No need to go to Manila. You have a nice girl now. You don't need army."

* * *

At 7:45 a.m. the next day, September 7, 1941, Colonel Blake arrived at Zenji's house to drive him to the harbor.

Zenji had packed his few clothes in an old suitcase and a duffel bag that the colonel had given him. No uniform or military papers, nothing to link him to the army.

Henry, Aiko, and Ma walked Zenji out to the street. Henry had taken the day off, his first ever. "Be brave, little brother," he said, putting both hands on Zenji's shoulders. "When you're afraid, don't show it. Make your family proud . . . for Pop. Be like him, and Ma. Tough! Tough is *good*! Tough like the great samurai, like me!" Henry tried to laugh, but couldn't.

Zenji gazed deep into Henry's eyes, wanting him to see, to know without question that he would *never* bring shame on his family or his country. "Fear will never control me, big brother."

Henry nodded.

When they reached the car, Ma finally broke down. "My son, my son," she said, her eyes filled with tears. "I know there is no war . . . but there is *talk* of war, everywhere. I'm afraid for you, Zenji-*kun*."

"Don't worry, Ma, I—"

She put her hand up to stop him. "Shhh."

He nodded, and looked deep into her eyes.

Aiko hooked her arm in Zenji's and laid her head on his shoulder. Henry pulled Ma close.

"Remember this," Ma said, standing tall. "Your father and his brothers all served in the Japanese Army. You must be like them. Wherever you go and whatever you do, serve your country with courage and honor."

Zenji knew what she was saying: Death is more acceptable

than cowardice. Nothing is more important than the honor of the family. Do not bring shame upon the Watanabe name.

Zenji took his mother's hands in his. "No matter what happens, Ma, there's no way I'll return in disgrace. I promise you."

She patted his shoulder, the closest she would come to showing affection outside the house. "Come home to us, Zenji-*kun*."

"I will, Ma. Please don't worry about me."

Ma pressed a folded piece of paper into his hand. "Read later."

Zenji stuck the note in his pocket. The weight in his heart was almost unbearable. He hugged her, right out in the open.

Then Zenji hugged Aiko, squeezing her tight. "Stay close to Ma," he whispered. "She's strong, but she'll need you. Save her poems, too, so I can read them when I get back."

"And when will that be?"

"Next blue moon?" He smiled.

"Don't say that!"

"I'll write you, and you write back, okay? *Lots* of letters! Tell me everything you do. I'm going to miss you!"

"Zenji—I put some of Mina's pie in your bag. I wrapped it really well, and . . ."

He hugged her hard. "You're the best."

He shook hands with Henry, gave him a quick embrace. They stood back and looked at each other. They didn't need words.

Zenji turned to Colonel Blake. "I'm ready, sir."

Colonel Blake touched his forehead in a two-finger salute to Henry. He bowed to Aiko and Ma.

As they drove away, Zenji looked back one last time.

Henry and Ma stood straight and still, Henry with an arm around Ma's shoulders.

Only Aiko waved.

The colors, sounds, and smells of his neighborhood poured in through the car window as they drove toward his mysterious new life. For the first time he understood the saying "You never know what you have until you lose it."

Still, he was traveling to a new world.

He wished he'd asked Mina for her address. She'd wanted to write, but to where? He'd find a way to send her his address when he got it. He couldn't stop thinking about her. She was so easy to be with, and she cared about him.

Zenji pinched the bridge of his nose and closed his eyes. *Was* he doing the right thing?

"Doing okay, Zenji?"

"Yes, sir. But . . . I'm going to miss my family and . . . and my friends."

"Of course."

It was exciting, but also strange. Didn't all soldiers need some basic skills first, like Henry's friends were getting at Schofield Barracks? All he had were his orders: ship out.

Good thing he'd trained in JROTC.

"Colonel, how come I'm not going to boot camp first like everyone else?"

"You'll get the training you need in Manila. Remember, your work will be different."

"Right, thank you."

Ahead, the harbor was light green and flat as a pond. Zenji

snorted. I wanted to travel and see the world, and now my palms are sweating. He wiped them on his pants.

The colonel glanced at him. "You take care of yourself in Manila, Zenji. Use your head."

"I will, sir."

"You have a good future ahead of you, and I'll be here to help you when you get back."

Zenji looked at the colonel, trying to let him know how grateful he was. "I'll always remember what you taught me, sir."

Colonel Blake nodded and turned down the road to the pier.

13
COVER STORY

The wharf buzzed with activity—people, trucks, forklifts. Zenji could see the warehouse where he'd worked.

They parked and sat looking at the two ships alongside the pier. One was Zenji's.

The colonel dipped his head toward them. "Make your way on board without being conspicuous. Act like an ordinary traveler. They're expecting you. Someone will meet you on deck and tell you what to do."

The colonel glanced in the rearview mirror. "From here on out you want to be anonymous."

"Yes, sir . . . but why?"

The colonel smiled for the first time that morning. "It will all make sense soon."

Zenji got out. He grabbed his suitcase and duffel, set them

down, and looked back in at Colonel Blake. "Thank you for everything, sir. I appreciate it."

The colonel reached over and shook Zenji's hand. His grip was strong. "Remember, Zenji. Pay close attention to your instructions, then follow them unfailingly. Be invisible. Don't put yourself in danger. Trust your instincts. Trust *yourself*. Be alert. Every second. Got it?"

"Listen carefully, be invisible, don't put myself in danger, follow instructions, trust myself. And get back here in one piece! And, sir, can you check in on my family while I'm gone? Once in a while?"

"Of course. I'll write and let you know how they are."

The colonel squeezed Zenji's hand and let go.

"Another thing," he added, tapping his forehead. "Take care of this. If war does come you will see some things you won't want to see, and you can't let it get to you. Block it out. Harden yourself. Think of your family. Think of every good thing you can. You come home to us."

Zenji studied him. War?

Two plus two equals four, little brother.

"I'll do my best, sir. Count on it. No matter what happens."

"I know you will."

Zenji shouldered his duffel, grabbed his suitcase, and headed toward the pier without looking back.

Hundreds of soldiers waited in a long, lazy line to board the ship, army gear stacked everywhere. The men talked, laughed, shouted, and sang, as if they were going on vacation.

Zenji found a dockworker who told him that the *Republic* was the ship going to Manila.

Zenji casually headed up the gangway.

A man dressed as a civilian approached. "Watanabe?"

Haole, looked like a businessman. Aloha shirt, khaki pants, and leather shoes.

"Yes."

"Come with me, please."

He led Zenji down steel stairs to a stateroom eight feet long and five feet wide, with two bunks on one side.

"Top rack is yours. Your roommate got here first."

A suitcase and duffel were stashed under the lower bunk.

"Who's my roommate?"

"Kid from Maui, Kimura."

Zenji shook his head. "Don't know him."

The guy smirked. "In these quarters you'll know each other extremely well by the time you get to the Philippines."

"I'll bet."

A young Japanese guy ducked through the door. "Hey, you must be the wonder boy I been hearing about. You Watanabe?"

"That's me. Name's Zenji."

"Freddy Kimura." He reached out to shake with a smile. "We took that test together, remember?"

"Yeah, sure," Zenji said, but he didn't. There were so many guys.

"Okay, listen up," the haole said. "This is important. I'm CIP, just like you two. That's Corps of Intelligence Police. For security reasons we won't be seeing much of each other on this bucket. The first thing you need to know is that you've been transferred from the Hawaiian Detachment, U.S. Army, to the Philippine Detachment, U.S. Army. You've been assigned to G2. The '2' means intelligence."

Zenji listened intently, remembering the G2 on Colonel Sutherland's office door at Fort Shafter. He glanced at Freddy, who raised his eyebrows and grinned. "Spies."

The CIP guy went on.

"To everyone else on this ship you're basically nobodies. Civilian travelers. Keep a low profile and don't talk to anyone about anything other than the weather. If you have to say something to avoid suspicion, your cover story is that you are just two guys heading to Manila to look for work. Fraternize with no one. Besides myself, only the ship's captain and someone you'll meet later on know who you are. Any questions?"

"Yeah," Freddy said. "Where's the girls' deck?"

"Wise guy."

"I have a question," Zenji said. "Do we need fake names, or what?"

"No. Use your real name. You start using a fake one, and somebody checks, they'll get suspicious. You're just two American civilians heading to an American commonwealth looking for work. However, you will each have a code name for security purposes."

Freddy looked at Zenji and winked.

"You," the CIP guy said to Freddy. "Your code name is *Spider.* When someone calls you that, you answer, *Hate those things.* That way you will both know the other is legitimate. Understand?"

"Clear as mud."

"Yeah, and you," he said, turning to Zenji. "Your code name is *Bamboo Rat.* When someone calls you that, you answer with *I heard they live underground.* Got it?"

Zenji nodded.

"Any more questions?"

Zenji had a thousand. He shook his head.

"Good. I hope you don't get seasick."

The CIP guy left.

"I guess we made it, then," Freddy said.

"Made what?"

"It's official—we're certified nobodies."

Zenji grinned. "Spider, huh?"

"Hate those things. You look like a bamboo rat."

"I heard they live underground."

Freddy shook his head. "Crazy."

"How do they come up with these names?" Zenji said.

"Search their nightmares."

They laughed, and went up on deck to stand at the rail, looking down on the troops heading aboard in a long, slow-moving line. Each carried a huge backpack and a duffel.

Zenji pointed with his chin. "Where are these guys from?"

"New Mexico. Army Reserves. I asked them."

"You asked? That's not being invisible."

"Those guys don't care. Look at them. All they're thinking is, where are the hula girls? This is Hawaii, right?"

Some did look kind of disappointed. Zenji nodded toward a figure in the crowd on the pier. "Look. Sutherland."

He wanted to wave, but that wouldn't be invisible.

Freddy humphed. "I guess he wanted to make sure we got on board."

Colonel Sutherland looked up, giving no indication that he saw either of them.

So weird.

"Who are we supposed to be hiding from, anyway?"

Freddy winked again and whispered, "Spies."

"What spies?"

"The ones we're hiding from."

Zenji grunted. "What school did you go to?"

"St. Anthony on Maui, then over here at the university. What about you?"

"McKinley."

"Tokyo High, right? Almost all Japanese?"

"That's what they call it."

"You still look like high school. How old are you, anyway?"

"Not old enough to be in the army. I had to get my mom's permission."

Freddy raised an eyebrow. "They wanted you pretty bad."

"I guess."

"Cannon fodder."

"What's that mean?"

"It means you better get good at digging foxholes."

A couple of hours later, two tugs pushed the *Republic* out into the harbor. Zenji and Freddy stayed at the rail to watch as the ship slowly powered out to sea.

Zenji gazed back at his island. When would he see it again?

"How long you think it'll take us to get to Manila, Freddy?"

"Two weeks, I heard."

Zenji glanced toward the distant horizon. "What will we find there, I wonder?"

"Filipinos."

"Are you ever serious?"

"Not if I can help it."

"Good." He and Freddy Kimura were going to get along fine, even in an eight-by-five-foot room.

Freddy waved to the island. "Bye-bye, hula girls."

Men stood all along the rail, silently watching the island shrink. The ship's engines thrummed, an exciting yet calming sound.

Zenji remembered Ma's note and pulled it from his pocket. He curled it into his closed fist.

Long minutes later, he unfolded it.

He looked at her familiar Kanji.

When
Tomorrow starts
Without you here,
So begins my prayer
For your honorable
And safe
Return.

His ears tingled.

Oh, Ma . . .

LUSH GREEN ISLAND

Fifteen long, boring days later, the *Republic* drew within three miles of Manila Bay. Zenji and Freddy had spent the trip walking from one end of the ship to the other, practicing eavesdropping, observing people, and slipping out of sight, trying not to be seen. Zenji caught Freddy more times than Freddy caught him.

"Got to get better at your spycraft," Zenji said.

"Maybe we're not going to be spies."

"Then why are we hiding from each other?"

"Because we're bored out of our minds?"

Zenji punched Freddy's arm. What a wise guy. He liked him as much as Tosh.

As they approached the harbor, Zenji, Freddy, and every last man on the ship surged to the rails to gaze at the lush, green land with a coast that went on forever.

"This is an island?" Zenji asked.

"Luzon."

Even at a distance he could smell the earth, and almost taste the rich thickness of salty tropical air born of shallow waters.

"The Pearl of the Orient," he whispered.

Freddy whistled, low. "Almost as nice as where we came from, ah?"

Zenji agreed . . . but new thoughts were starting up. About machetes. Murders in the night. Ma's words had scratched their way into the darkest corners of his mind.

Stop! Thinking like this will drive you crazy!

Still . . .

He nudged Freddy. "You think Filipinos carry machetes here?"

Freddy looked at him and burst out laughing. "Machetes! For a minute I thought you were serious."

"No, no . . . just joking."

Freddy kept chuckling. "Chop-chop."

"Hey you!" someone behind them called.

They turned to see the CIP guy. Zenji had forgotten all about him.

"You boys enjoy your trip?"

"Yeah," Freddy said. "But it was too short."

The CIP guy snorted. "Follow me."

Zenji tried to hide his excitement. Finally he and Freddy would learn why they were so important. The army didn't go through testing and bringing them here just to have them read newspapers and listen to the radio. There had to be more.

The CIP guy led them up steel stairs to the bridge. It was deserted, except for a gray-haired man and the ship's captain.

The CIP guy motioned them toward the gray-haired man, who was studying a nautical chart. "This is Major Thomas Harding, G2 operations officer, U.S. Army, Philippines Detachment. Your new boss."

"Sir," Zenji said.

Should he shake hands or salute? He chose to salute.

"None of that," the major snapped. "Not with what you'll be doing."

"And what's that?" Freddy asked boldly.

The major pulled two envelopes from his coat pocket and handed one to each of them. "You'll find everything you need to know in these envelopes. But don't open them now. You can do that onshore while you travel to your respective destinations."

Zenji glanced at Freddy. "We're not going to the same place?"

"The instructions will explain everything. Right now, we need to get you off this ship secretly. We don't want any Philippine government officials to be able to identify you as having come in with all these troops, so we're going to get you off before we dock."

Freddy grinned. "I like it."

The ship's captain nodded to Major Harding. "The launch."

The CIP guy hooked a finger toward Zenji and Freddy. "Time to pack up."

Zenji hesitated, looking at the major.

"Be careful disembarking," the major said. "The launch will let you off in a secluded spot. Once onshore, read your instructions, then split up and catch a cab to your destinations. Make sure it's a Yellow Cab. The others can be unpredictable. Act like you know the place. Never look at a map in public. You'll stand out like the blinking lights on an ambulance."

They left the bridge.

Freddy and Zenji grabbed their gear and the CIP guy took them to a part of the ship where the crew had fashioned a view shield and hung a rope ladder over the side.

Zenji looked down to the water.

Below, a burly Filipino stared up from a small launch. He was holding just off the hull of the ship, keeping pace as the *Republic* eased toward the harbor.

It was a long way down. And the ship wasn't going to stop.

Zenji stepped back. "It looks dangerous."

"It *is* dangerous, if you don't focus on what you're doing," the CIP guy said. "Just take it slow and easy. We'll lower your gear down after you. Just don't fall in the water. The screw on this tub will eat you alive."

"The screw?" Zenji said.

"The propeller. It'll suck you right under and chop you up. Not a good way to go."

Zenji's hands trembled all the way down the loose rope ladder. It was the scariest thing he'd ever done in his life. Once he was safely in the small boat, he took a deep breath, amazed at what he'd just accomplished.

"That wasn't bad," he said when Freddy plopped down in the launch next to him.

"Piece of cake."

The Filipino who skippered the launch was silent as he gathered their gear and secured it under the seats.

"What's your name?" Freddy asked.

The Filipino looked up.

"Name," Freddy repeated.

The guy rapid-fired some incomprehensible response, waving in the direction of the island. Then he laughed and headed over to the controls.

Zenji elbowed Freddy "You get all that?"

"Sure. He said last time he did this a guy fell in the water and the sharks got him. He's looking forward to seeing that happen again. Maybe today."

"Sharks?" Zenji glanced at the water.

"Man, you Honolulu boys are so gullible."

"Not."

Freddy shielded his mouth with his hand and whispered, "Watch out. He just picked up his machete." He cracked up as the Filipino hit the throttle. The bow rose up out of the water, and flattened when the launch got up to speed and raced toward the mysterious island of Luzon.

15

THE MOMO

The Filipino skipper took them to a small deserted beach park. He tossed their gear onto the sand and buzzed back out into the bay without a word.

In the distance, the *Republic* steamed into Manila Bay.

Zenji threw his duffel over his shoulder and grabbed his suitcase. "I don't think that guy liked us."

Freddy grunted.

They found a grassy spot in a small grove of palm trees where they dropped their gear and sat.

Zenji took out his envelope.

Freddy slapped his against his palm.

Zenji knew how he felt. He wasn't eager to open his, either.

"This is one of those moments," Freddy said. "Once we read what's in here our lives will shoot off in new directions. The question is, will we like it?"

"We have to."

"Welcome to the army, ah?"

Zenji tore his envelope open and pulled out a half page of written instructions.

And cash—U.S. dollars and Filipino pesos.

And a small key to a post office mailbox, number 72.

He looked up at Freddy.

Freddy shrugged. "That's all I got, too."

Sure wasn't much after all they'd gone through to get here.

Zenji stuffed the key and the cash into his pants pocket and read the letter.

Follow these instructions exactly. Commit them to memory and destroy this communiqué immediately after reading.

Make your way by cab to a Japanese-owned hotel called the Momo. Ask for a room using your real name. There will be vacancy. Guests there are almost all businessmen from Japan. The hotel serves good Japanese food, which is why the businessmen stay there.

You are to use the enclosed key at the Central Post Office in Manila twice a day for your daily orders and information. Your first visit to the mailbox will be Thursday morning by 0900 hours.

Under no circumstances are you to reveal your connection with the U.S. military. You are a civilian—repeat: civilian—looking for work abroad. Nothing else.

Further instructions will await you at the post office.
Destroy this communiqué now.

They compared letters. The only difference was the mailbox number and hotel. Freddy's was called the Toyo.

"Looks like we really are supposed to be spies," Freddy said.

"No, we're translators. What do we know about spying? And what's there to spy on?"

Freddy shrugged. "Who cares? Whatever we're doing, I like it so far."

"It's mysterious, in a spooky way."

"An adventure, city boy. Climb aboard."

Zenji shook his head, fingering the key in his pocket. Just a month ago he was goofing off with Aiko and Nami. Now look. Ma would've croaked if she'd seen him climbing off that ship.

"Well," Freddy said, reaching out to shake. "Guess this is it."

"For now, anyway." Zenji took his hand. "If you need me, I'm at the Momo hotel. And you're at the Toyo."

Freddy grinned. "I hope it has a swimming pool."

They nodded once, then let go and turned toward the ocean for one last look. The *Republic* was out of sight, the sea smooth and quiet, as if nothing had ever disturbed it.

"Onward," Zenji said, turning back. "Good luck, Spider."

"Hate those things."

"Me too."

"Chop-chop."

Freddy walked away laughing, his duffel on his shoulder and his suitcase dangling from his hand.

Zenji tore his letter into tiny pieces and buried them in five different holes he dug deep in the sand. It would be quite a puzzle for anyone to find the pieces and put them back together.

He headed through the trees in the direction Freddy had gone. When he reached the road that edged the shoreline, he looked back to be sure he hadn't been followed.

He was alone.

He saw Freddy in the distance, walking toward Manila, and waited until he caught a cab before moving out into the open.

A few cars passed. None of the drivers paid any attention to him.

About fifteen minutes later, he spotted a cab and flagged it down. The driver's name was Carlo and he spoke decent English.

"Where you like go, mistah?"

"Uh . . . Momo hotel?" Zenji said, too fast. *Slow down.* It was his first time in a taxi. He knew at the end you had to pay, but that was it.

Carlo glanced up at the rearview mirror as they sped away. "Whatchoo doing way out here?"

"Somebody dropped me off. They had to get home."

Carlo nodded.

Zenji cringed. What a dumb answer! He'd have to get better at making stuff up.

They headed into the city.

Manila was far busier than Honolulu. They drove past cramped huts and through old streets, across a river, into a city edged by parks and big homes that were hidden by hedges and rich landscaping. The contrast was startling. Poor, then wealthy. Crowded, then spacious. Frantic, then peaceful.

The drive along the sparkling bay was lined with palm trees, and Zenji could almost see himself at home in Hawaii.

"Momo," Carlo said, startling Zenji out of his daydream. "Nice hotel. I had dinner there once."

"Uh, yeah . . . the food is why I stay there."

"Lot of you guys stay there."

"You guys?"

"Japanese."

"Yeah, yeah. We like it."

It wasn't part of his cover story, but he figured he didn't have to explain anything to a cabdriver.

They drove on. Manila air flowed into the cab, hot and humid.

Carlo kept peeking up at the rearview mirror.

Zenji caught him looking, but quickly averted his eyes. Already this undercover stuff was getting to him. He needed to work on getting comfortable with it. If he felt nervous, he'd look nervous. Which would bring unwanted attention.

"Nice day," Zenji said. That sounded okay. Normal.

"Hot," Carlo answered.

The guy didn't look Filipino, Zenji thought. Maybe he was Spanish. Back home at the library he'd read that Spain had once claimed these islands. The architecture of the buildings was kind of Spanish, too.

Grass, trees, a river running through the city. Shiny cars, people walking around in loose shirts, bare feet, slippers, shorts. Bicycles, carts. In some spots it could even be Honolulu.

Zenji nodded. He was going to like it here.

He leaned forward and pulled his sweaty shirt away from his back, wishing he had shorts on. "Humid."

Carlo looked into the rearview mirror. "Even if you doing nothing, you sweat. Best place is a seat in a bar . . . by a fan." He laughed.

"I'll remember that."

At the hotel, Zenji pulled his gear out. He paid Carlo and added a generous tip. "Thanks for the ride," he said, and bowed for good measure.

Carlo looked at Zenji a moment too long.

"What?" Zenji said.

"For Japanese, you seem diff'rent. Not bossy. And you bowed. Firs' one I ever met did that to me." The guy dipped his head and drove off with a smile.

Zenji watched him go, then turned toward the hotel.

Here goes nothing.

The Momo wasn't deluxe, but it was very well kept.

The five Japanese businessmen sitting in the lobby glanced over the top of their newspapers when Zenji walked in with his suitcase and duffel.

Zenji nodded and headed to the counter. He felt instantly out of place. He was at least ten years younger than the youngest man there.

"I . . . uh, I'd like a room," Zenji said in Japanese.

The Japanese hotel clerk waited a long moment before answering. "You don't have a reservation?"

"No, sir, I don't. But do you have a room?"

The man opened a book, turned a few pages. "Hmm," he said, shaking his head.

Zenji wondered why. It wasn't that big of a hotel. Twenty-five rooms, at most, and he didn't know if he had a vacancy?

"Where you from?" the guy asked, looking up.

"Honolulu."

That got a reaction. "Honolulu? Your family live there?"

"Yes. I'm Nisei."

The guy's face lit up. "Hey," he called to the guys in the lobby. "This kid is from Honolulu. He's Nisei."

Zenji turned.

All five businessmen folded their papers and headed over, as if being a second-generation American was something amazing.

"None of us has ever met an American Nisei before," the clerk said. "What are you doing here?"

The businessmen gathered around the counter. They didn't seem threatening. Then Zenji thought: well, why would they?

He had to loosen up.

"I had a job on a ship," Zenji said. "But I decided I wanted to work on land. I get kind of seasick."

The businessmen laughed.

One guy asked, "Where did your family come from?"

"Okinawa. My parents moved to Hawaii to find work. But my father was killed in an accident. I live with my mother, brother, and sister."

The hotel guy nodded thoughtfully.

"And," Zenji added, getting better at making stuff up, "I was, uh, about to get called up by the army. I didn't want that, so I got a job on the ship. But the ship, like I said, made me seasick. I thought Manila seemed like a good place to, uh, you know, find work."

"It is," the clerk said with a smile.

Zenji looked down. What a story he'd just told! Where had all that come from? It was so easy to make up.

"I didn't want to leave home," he added, getting into it. "But my mother didn't want me in the army, so she let me travel."

Maybe he should shut up. But everyone nodded, seeming to understand his predicament.

"How old are you?" the hotel guy asked.

"Twenty-one."

The clerk grunted and reached out to shake. "Call me Tadeo. I own the place."

The clerk owned the hotel? Ho, Zenji thought. He would have to start judging people better.

Zenji shook Tadeo's hand. "So, do you have a room?"

"Sure. How long you want to stay?"

"A while, I guess. I have some money."

After he signed in, Zenji spent the next half hour talking with the men in the lobby. It was the first time in his life that he'd been a curiosity, and he kind of liked it. They were friendly and made him feel at home.

But that night in his room, he was overcome by emotion, lonely and homesick for his family and all that he had known up to now.

His throat swelled. He wished Freddy were around to

cheer him up. Even the noisy geckos outside reminded him of home.

But in the following days the Japanese businessmen treated Zenji like a younger brother, someone to mentor and advise. Zenji liked these guys.

Soon his homesickness vanished, and he didn't even notice the noisy geckos anymore. They were just part of the night, like cars passing on the streets, or music from nearby nightclubs. It surprised and pleased him how easily he could burrow into the landscape of Manila.

The Bamboo Rat had arrived.

16
FIRST CONTACT

For the next few days, Zenji wandered around, getting a feel for the city. On Thursday at nine a.m., he took his key to the post office and checked mailbox number 72.

Inside was a single envelope.

He folded it twice, stuck it in his pocket.

He'd read it in a more private place. He locked the mailbox. Before he left he bought a postcard with an aerial shot of Manila on it.

What would a civilian do? Someone who just got here? Be relaxed, for a start. He had to start building his cover.

He sat in a park and wrote to Aiko, giving her the address of the Momo. He told her he was fine, that he missed everyone, and that he liked it in Manila. There were nice people here. *And tell Ma I haven't seen a machete yet. That's a joke,*

Aiko. And one more thing—can you ask Tosh to give Mina my address?

Since he was supposed to be a civilian, he had no concern about revealing his location. In fact, if anyone checked, it just strengthened his story.

He mailed the card.

The day was hot and very humid, and the folded letter in his pocket was on his mind.

He found a fountain shaded by a banyan tree and sat on a bench. No one seemed to be watching him, as far as he could tell. Being at the Momo under false pretenses did make him a kind of spy, even though he didn't know what he was supposed to be spying on.

Relax. Breathe.

He cleaned his glasses with his shirt.

It suddenly hit him that Manila could be crawling with spies from Japan . . . who were watching *him*!

Nah. Doesn't make sense.

He put his glasses back on. Trying hard to be inconspicuous, he took the folded envelope from his pocket and eased it open.

Be at the corner of Magallanes and Padre Burgos at 1400 hours. Look for a white sedan.

Zenji checked his watch. Plenty of time.

He glanced up the street and around the fountain. Nothing looked out of the ordinary. He tore the note into tiny shreds and dropped the pieces into two different trash cans as he headed out to find that corner.

If only he could look at a map! He had one in his room, and he'd studied it well. Still, it would probably take all the time he had to find the right streets.

He'd have to rely on dumb luck.

He found the intersection with a half hour to spare.

The sidewalks were busy, which was good. He could blend in.

He leaned against a post near a crowded bus stop and pretended he was waiting for a bus. Perfect.

At two o'clock a white car stopped. The driver scanned the sidewalk.

Zenji stepped forward.

The driver motioned him over. He looked American. "Bamboo Rat?" he asked.

"I heard they live underground."

"Get in."

Zenji nodded and slid into the front seat, relieved.

The guy checked his side-view mirror and pulled back into traffic. "Warm enough for you?"

He wasn't in uniform, but he had the same military posture as Colonel Blake. Short hair, focused attention.

"Heat's okay," Zenji said. "It's the humidity."

"Sucks the life right out of you."

"What is a bamboo rat, anyway?" Zenji asked. "You ever seen one?"

"Over in Burma, I did. Like a massive hamster, and they actually do live underground. They're pests. They eat bamboo roots and kill the plant. Wipe out entire forests. Lots of weird creatures down here."

"Pests."

The guy laughed. "It's just a code name. But here's the funny thing: there aren't any bamboo rats in the Philippines. You're the only one."

"Where we going?"

"G2 headquarters, Fort Santiago. Look around as we drive so you can find your way on your own if you ever have to. It's pretty easy. Just head north and then toward the bay when you hit the river."

After a short drive, they turned into a massive stone entry gate and pulled up to a security shack. The driver showed his ID. The guard glanced at it, peeked in at Zenji, and waved them through.

They pulled up in front of a three-story building.

"This is it," the driver said. "Look for the office of Colonel Jake Olsten. He's the head of G2."

Zenji got out. "Thanks for the ride."

The guy grinned and drove off.

Maybe now Zenji would get some real answers.

As Zenji walked in, the colonel stood, smiled, and reached across his desk to shake. "Colonel Olsten. Welcome to G2."

"Zenji Watanabe, sir."

"Everything going well since you arrived?"

"Yes, sir. Everything's fine."

"And the hotel?"

"Nice people, and the food's good."

Colonel Olsten nodded. "Been there myself. Please, sit down."

First, Colonel Olsten told Zenji what his military pay would be: eighty dollars a month. Jeese. Henry was right: peanuts. Not even half of what he'd made at the warehouse in Honolulu.

"I know," the colonel said, reading Zenji's face. "It doesn't sound like much, but there are benefits. You'll also receive a generous food and clothing allowance, and you'll be reimbursed for expenses while doing your job. Theoretically, you can save every penny you make."

"Sounds fine, sir. I need to send my pay home."

"We can work that out."

"Thank you, sir. What's my job? Japanese radio? Translating documents? The kind of stuff I did in Honolulu?"

"There's that. But there's more. First of all—and this is utterly important for your safety, and your cover—never, ever have anything even remotely related to the military on your person or in your possession at any time, even in your hotel room. Is that clear?"

"Yes, sir," Zenji said, his nerves going into overdrive.

"You noticed that we didn't exchange salutes when you walked in?"

"Oh, sorry. I—"

The colonel held up a hand. "I don't *want* you to salute. It's a dead giveaway, and I mean *dead*. Never, ever salute."

"Uh . . . yes, sir."

"And don't say *sir*, either. *Ever*."

"Okay."

Colonel Olsten grinned. "That said, you are now a special undercover agent, United States Military Intelligence. You know your code name, right?"

"Bamboo Rat."

"And the response?"

"I heard they live underground."

"And you have your cover story down?"

"I'm just a civilian, looking for work."

Colonel Olsten tapped his desk to punctuate the point. "Perfect. An American civilian in an American commonwealth."

"That's me."

"Now," Colonel Olsten went on, "you will receive periodic instructions and file your reports by way of your mailbox. Check twice a day. To maintain your cover, we've secured a job for you. Not a real job, a cover job, which you'll understand once you go there. Even though the job isn't real, it's extremely important that you show up. We need people to trust you and to believe you are who you say you are."

Zenji listened carefully. "Where's the job?"

"International Trading Company. An American business that's been cooperating with us."

How could you have a fake job and make it look real?

Colonel Olsten went on. "Here's what you will really be doing." He got up and started to pace. "There's a lot at stake here. Our relations with Japan are getting worse. We're trying to negotiate a peaceful coexistence, but personally I'm not optimistic. They need our oil and we're not giving it to them. We're also worried that Japan and Germany are about to cause us even more concern. There's no telling where *that* would lead."

"I heard back home that Japan was causing trouble in China," Zenji said. "But the Japanese businessmen at the hotel are friendly. They treat me well. They don't seem like they could kill innocent people."

"There's a big difference between civilian Japan and military Japan. Now listen, your assignment is to live among and mingle with the Japanese nationals in Manila, several of whom you are already acquainted with at the hotel. We need you to observe and identify anyone you suspect might be working for Japanese military intelligence. I can't put my finger on exactly what might allow you to know that, but I want to know about anything that stirs your curiosity. Listen in on conversations. Look for the unusual. Talk with the men at your hotel, see what they say, try to discern what they think. Pay particular attention to anyone asking a lot of questions. *Anything and everything, you bring it to me.*"

Zenji shifted, beginning to feel the weight of what was expected of him. It's true. Freddy was right.

"You mean I'll be a . . . spy?"

The colonel clapped his hand on Zenji's shoulder and looked him in the eye. "Starting with the nationals at the Momo hotel."

Zenji opened his mouth to speak.

But nothing came out.

"We'll have a man at the International Trading Company talk to you on your first day. He'll give you a few pointers on how to observe without being noticed. But you'll see him only once. We can't risk having the two of you seen together more than that. It'll have to do."

Spy on the men at the Momo.

Back at the hotel Zenji sat on the edge of his bed and stared at the wall, thinking about the turn his life had just taken. What Colonel Olsten was saying was that those guys were no longer his friends and big brothers . . . they were his targets.

For their friendship, advice, help, and guidance, what he would give them in return wouldn't be appreciation and gratitude. It would be betrayal.

It took his breath away.

RUMORS OF WAR

Early the next day Zenji checked his map and slipped out of the Momo before any of the businessmen got up. He took what he hoped was an inconspicuous route to his new fake job in a warehouse near the harbor.

He stopped once to look into a store window, studying the reflection of what was behind him on the street. It didn't seem that anyone was following him.

He frowned. Why would anyone follow me? Is there more going on here than I can see?

He chewed on that for a moment, then continued on. Was Freddy doing the same thing and having the same thoughts?

Boy, he sure missed him and his jokes. Where are you, Spider? Are you betraying good guys, too?

The businessmen at the Momo were generous with him. Talking with them at dinner the night before had gone well enough, though the joy Zenji had felt in their camaraderie had been drained away. That was the hard part. Living the lie, the pretense.

He jammed his hands into his pockets.

Get used to it. It's your duty.

The warehouse was similar to the one he'd worked in at home. A man was waiting for him. Just a regular-looking guy in a beige suit.

"Bamboo Rat?"

"I heard they live underground."

He pulled Zenji to a private corner and spoke fast. "If anyone asks, you work here moving inventory. But it's just a front. Show up around nine each weekday. Enter by the front door, hang around for an hour or so, and sneak out the back."

"Then what?" Zenji asked.

The guy looked over his shoulder. They were alone. "Educate yourself. Roam the city. Learn your way around. Check in at the post office and follow the instructions you get. Most of all, learn to notice things. Notice everything."

"What about training? I didn't even go to boot camp."

The guy snorted. "This *is* boot camp. Listen, we're learning as we go. You're the Bamboo Rat, right? Creep around at night, live underground? That's what you do."

Be invisible. Sure.

"The bottom line is we need information about what Japan's up to," the guy went on. "Be aware of what's around you at all times. If we're spying on them, then we have to assume they're spying on us. If you're in a restaurant, sit with your back to a wall, with a clear line of sight to the entrance and exits. Don't ever go to your destination directly. Always take a confusing route—that's why you need to learn the city. Your job is to keep an eye on Japanese nationals, see what they do, where they go. Listen in on conversations. Stay in the background. Notice anything out of place. You'll get the hang of it. Pretty basic. If you hear anything out of the ordinary, especially anything military, we need to know about it. But never contact G2 directly. Never go there unless you're told to. Always use the post office."

"Like write a report?"

"Just note your observations, slip it into your mailbox, and get out of there. Got it?"

"Uh . . . yeah."

The guy nodded and left.

Zenji was on his own.

Zenji worked on his cover by using his allowance to buy clothes, shoes, and other things necessary to a young foreigner settling into a new job in Manila.

The guys at the Momo enjoyed hearing about what life was like in Hawaii so much that they often corralled him and bought him dinner. Now, when they talked about their lives back home, he listened with new ears.

It's your duty, he kept repeating to himself.

One evening, the subject of China came up. It was after dinner, and there were eight of them sitting around the table drinking rice wine.

"It's all about natural resources," one guy, Usui, said,

explaining Japan's situation to Zenji. "We just don't have them. We need oil, steel, and rubber. We have to buy that stuff."

"What does that have to do with China?" Zenji asked, wanting to keep the conversation alive, and also, he was curious. He truly didn't know.

"Well," Usui said, "they wouldn't sell those resources to us. They think we're getting too strong. So we had to go out and get them. That's why we're in China."

"You mean, you just went in and took them?"

The men looked at Zenji.

"What?" he said.

Usui steepled his fingertips. "You can be forgiven. After all, you *are* American."

The other men laughed, and Zenji breathed a sigh of relief. The last thing he needed to do was raise suspicion.

"What else were we going to do?" Usui went on. "China doesn't want us to grow stronger, so they keep their resources to themselves. Meanwhile, we suffer."

He leaned forward and looked closely at Zenji. "You guys don't like us getting stronger, either, so you also limit what we can buy. I mean, really, you're forcing us to fight for our existence."

Zenji nodded, as if he saw the sense in what Usui was saying. He wanted to ask about Nanking, but thought better of it. But he did mention his encounter with the three guys in Chinatown.

"Buddhism saved me," he said. "I refused to fight, but I also refused to grovel my way out."

This they liked.

"Your parents have taught you well, Zenji. They've retained the values of their homeland. I'm sure they see the necessity of Japan's expansion for its own survival."

Zenji nodded. He wanted to add: Sure, I see that you need resources, but killing innocent Chinese to get them is not the way.

He listened as the men went on about scrap steel, oil, and rubber, and the problems in French Indochina. "Your President Roosevelt is making our lives very difficult," Usui said.

"I see," Zenji commiserated. "But we're talking, right? The U.S. and Japan?"

Usui nodded. "There is some small hope for an understanding. But I fear we're too far apart."

The other men mumbled, nodding.

Zenji could not see the sense of going into another country and taking what you couldn't buy. It was not the way he had been taught. It was not . . . Japanese. Where was the respect and honor in it?

He was beginning to see that there was a great difference between how Japanese in Japan saw the world and how Japanese living in the U.S. saw things.

"Well," he said. "I really hope our countries can work things out."

"Yes," Usui said.

He studied Zenji, his head cocked to one side. "Have you ever thought about moving back to Japan?"

"Well, not actually moving back, since I've never been there . . . but I did once think about studying Buddhism in Kyoto. I was considering becoming a priest."

"Noble," Usui said, and the rest of the men nodded in agreement. "Why did you change your mind?"

Zenji grinned. "I need more action."

The men roared with laughter and raised their glasses.

For the rest of the evening, Zenji just listened, praying that he hadn't said anything he shouldn't have.

18
BAD FEELINGS

Zenji walked Manila with new intent, watching people, listening in on conversations, asking innocent questions of store clerks, slowly picking up information.

One day it rained harder than usual, and he found himself under an awning with six chatty Japanese businessmen. Zenji pretended to be new to the city and they were more than happy to share their thoughts and opinions.

He learned that there were currently around two thousand Japanese nationals living in Manila. Most of them were shop owners and entrepreneurs, and it seemed that they got along fine with both Filipinos and Americans. They should, he thought, considering there was a huge American military presence in the Philippines. If any of the nationals he came across were secret agents, Zenji sure couldn't tell.

But one day he met a man who made him uneasy.

Zenji was eating a sandwich, sitting on a park bench in the shade when the guy passed by. He stopped, and came back.

Zenji looked up.

"American?" the guy asked.

Zenji hesitated, then nodded.

"Thought so. Me too. Name's John Jones."

He stuck his hand out.

Zenji reached up and shook. "Zenji Watanabe. Why did you think I was American?"

"Don't see nationals eating sandwiches. You military?"

Zenji shook his head. "Civilian." He looked at his lunch. Lesson learned: sandwiches give you away.

Jones grinned. "I lived in Japan for a while. I know the people, the language, and what they eat."

Zenji nodded.

"You sure you're not military? Hey, it's fine with me if you are."

"No, I just work here."

"Doing what?"

Zenji shrugged. "Warehouse." He lifted his sandwich. "Lunch break."

Jones raised his eyebrows.

He doesn't believe me, Zenji thought. "How about you?" he asked. "Are you military?"

"Ha!" John Jones barked. "Not on your life."

Weird answer.

Zenji went back to his sandwich.

"Hey," the guy said after a beat. "Gotta run. Good to meet you, Zenji. Maybe I'll see you around."

"Yeah. See you around."

Zenji watched the man walk away, not sure what to think of him.

In the afternoon he strolled around trying to increase his feel for the city and the people. Most Filipinos spoke English, along with Tagalog, their first language. The fact that Zenji was from Hawaii lit them up with questions. Many had relatives there or knew people who'd gone to the islands to work on the plantations.

Zenji took an immediate liking to the Filipinos. Ma would be surprised at how friendly they were. Manila was a busy, and peaceful, place.

Still, there were rumors.

Looming war was in every conversation.

One night after dinner at the Momo, Zenji sat with eleven Japanese businessmen and Tadeo, the owner of the hotel.

"I have a bad feeling," Tadeo said.

Another man, Takahashi, asked why.

"I'm not very optimistic about the diplomatic talks."

Usui joined in. "Did you know that Ambassador Kurusu is replacing Nomura?"

"I heard." Tadeo thought a moment. "That's hopeful, I suppose. If anyone can negotiate with the Americans it would be Kurusu."

Usui turned to Zenji. "What do you think? As an American?"

Zenji sat up straighter and cleared his throat. "Well . . . all I know is what I read in the papers. Both sides seem to be communicating well enough, I guess." He had no idea if that was true or not.

"There you go," Takahashi said. "From America itself."

They laughed.

Tadeo held up a hand. "But you forget, America likes England, and the English are getting hammered by the Germans. The Americans might come to England's aid . . . and remember, Japan and Germany formed the 1936 alliance. Crazy."

"True, true."

They looked at Zenji, who shrugged and said, "I don't know much about politics and military stuff. But anything could happen, I guess." He shook his head thoughtfully.

His deception weighed on him more and more. If only he could dish answers out as easily as Freddy, like nothing was a big deal.

"Hey," he said, to change the subject. "You got a chessboard here? Anyone know how to play?"

For a moment no one spoke.

Then Tadeo slapped his knees and stood. "Of course. Why don't we see who has the better strategy? American or Japanese? You up for a game?"

Zenji smiled. What a relief! "Bring it on," he said, trying to remember the rules of chess. Lucky he used to play with Henry, although that was a few years ago.

Tadeo went to get the chess set.

Takahashi winked at Zenji. "I hope you know what you're doing. He takes his chess seriously."

"I used to be pretty good."

It would be a massacre.

But anything was better than questions.

THE UNDERWORLD

All through the rest of September and October 1941, Zenji roamed the city. If any Japanese nationals were doing anything out of the ordinary, he sure couldn't tell.

I'm so bad at this, he thought. They want a good spy, they should have trained me.

He tried to get information from reading Japanese newspapers in the hotel lobby, but he didn't find much that Colonel Olsten didn't already know.

However, the colonel was very interested in the conversations at the Momo hotel. "It's interesting that they seem perfectly fine with their occupation of Chinese territory. It's almost as if they feel they have a right to do whatever they want."

Zenji nodded. "I get that feeling, too."

"They believe they're racially superior to us, and all other races," Colonel Olsten said. "At least, their militaristic leaders do."

Zenji hesitated, thinking of how, in Hawaii, Japanese immigrants were looked poorly upon by those in power. And by other immigrants, too. "Don't . . . don't Americans also feel . . . you know, superior?"

"I suppose there's an ounce of truth to that, Zenji, but it doesn't drive us to attack other countries."

"True." He paused, trying to recall everything he'd learned by roaming around Manila. "Oh, there's something else. There was this guy a while back. He was American, so I didn't think to add him to my report . . . but I can't get him out of my mind."

Zenji told Colonel Olsten about his strange conversation with John Jones. "It felt like he was following me. I was uncomfortable around him. It was kind of creepy."

"Uncomfortable?"

"He kept asking me if I was in the military. I told him no, of course. And when I asked if *he* was in the military, he seemed offended. A very strange response."

Colonel Olsten studied Zenji a long moment. "Probably just curious. But if you run into him again, and he asks the same questions, I want to know about it. John Jones . . . sounds like a fake name."

Zenji was grateful that he had nothing significant to report about the friends he'd made at the hotel. "They seem to be exactly what they're supposed to be, Colonel Olsten. Businessmen with families back home. I can't even imagine them as spies."

"Don't let your feelings about these men get in the way of your judgment. If we go to war with Japan, everything changes."

"Right."

That night, Zenji lay awake. War with Japan? For what reason?

In the days that followed, his curiosity began to steer him farther and farther from the Momo hotel. He wanted to know more about Manila's people and its history. There was so much to see, so much to learn.

One day he found himself lost on an obscure backstreet packed with fruit and vegetable carts, open-backed trucks, and temporary booths bulging with goods of every kind. A river of people flowed in and out of the passageways, looking for bargains.

Zenji wasn't worried that he was lost. All he had to do was head toward the bay and he'd be able to find his way back to the hotel. Boy, he thought, moving along in the flow of human traffic, if I ever need to hide, this would be the place.

Around midafternoon he began to get a weird feeling. He didn't know why. He glanced around.

Nothing but everyday people cramming the streets.

Still, he felt as if he was being watched.

Or followed.

The hair on the back of his neck prickled.

Stop thinking! Who would follow you? You're nobody.

I'm the Bamboo Rat, he thought with an uneasy chuckle.

He worked his way to the edge of the flow, glancing back every once in a while to see if he could notice anything.

Nothing.

He decided to step into a shaded alcove and wait to see if anyone followed him in, or if anyone stopped when he stopped.

Minutes passed.

Nothing unusual.

This is nuts.

He was just about to head out when a hood fell over his head from behind. Somebody grabbed him and kicked the backs of his knees.

Zenji dropped like a stone.

A man shouted something that he didn't understand. Someone jammed a knee into his back and slammed him to the ground.

When he hit, the hood raised up enough for his exposed cheek to press into grit and oily pavement.

A man got down close to his ear and whispered something to him. Zenji didn't understand.

He tried to speak, but could only grunt. The pain in his back was excruciating.

Someone stole his watch. He could feel hands in his pockets, taking everything he had—money, hotel key, post office key, and the note Ma had given him on the day he left, which he carried with him at all times.

The guy spoke again.

"I don't understand you!" Zenji yelped, grimacing.

The guy punched his ear. Pain shot through his head like a lightning bolt.

There was a pause.

"English?" the man said, letting up on the pressure on Zenji's back.

Zenji gasped for air. "Amer . . . American."

The man slapped Zenji's head, once, twice. "No ID. Where ID?"

"I don't . . . have . . . one!"

The man slapped his head again.

Two men pulled him to his feet. They yanked the hood off. Zenji blinked, his scratched cheek stinging.

Four men surrounded him, coming in close, so close he could smell their sweat and see the blood vessels in their eyes.

Filipinos.

"What you doing here? American army?"

Zenji caught his breath. "No. I'm a civilian. I was just . . . walking around."

The leader grabbed Zenji's stuff from the guy who'd rifled through his pockets. The two other guys took over holding Zenji. "Where ID? You army?"

"No, not army. Civilian."

The guy counted the money, and looked at Ma's note. "American civilian?" he asked, still looking at the note. "This is Japanese? From your mama?"

"Yeah . . . I'm from Honolulu. You read Japanese?"

"Little bit." The guy jerked his chin at the two guys holding Zenji.

They let up on Zenji.

"Stupid, you come in here, English. You could die. Dangerous."

Zenji rubbed his face, trying to look grateful for the advice. He'd gotten the point. "Sorry."

The guy grunted and gave Zenji his stuff back, the keys, Ma's note . . . but not the money. He took that, counted it, kept half and waved the other half in Zenji's face. "You make me promise, I let you live. Deal?"

"Deal," Zenji said.

The guy jammed the money into Zenji's shirt pocket. "Send that home to your mama."

One of the other guys took a step closer and said something in a low voice.

The leader grinned. "He say he like carve his name in you belly. You smart, you go, fast."

Zenji's arms and legs buzzed with adrenaline. "I'm out of here. Gone."

The leader shoved him toward the street.

Zenji stumbled out of the alley into the sunlight. No one on the street looked at him. Zenji could tell that they were scared of the guys behind him.

The four guys followed several paces behind for close to ten minutes. When Zenji could no longer hear them, he glanced back and found them gone.

He stopped, leaned against a building, and bent over to throw up. No one stopped to ask if he needed help.

When he was able, he moved on toward the bay. His burning face and aching kidneys grew worse as he worked his way back to the Momo. Luckily, he made it to his room without being seen.

Ma's note, he thought, lying on his bed. That's what saved me.

He pulled the money out of his shirt pocket and looked at it. That money would end up in his mother's hands if it was the last thing he did.

* * *

106

The next time he was called in to see Colonel Olsten, Zenji told him about the incident in the ghetto. "You wandered into Freddy's territory," the colonel said. "He sees guys like that every day."

"And they don't kill him?"

"They pushed him around at first. But you know Freddy. He bounced back and made it a point to get to know them. Now they give him information, some of it valuable."

"Who *are* they?"

"Survivors. Criminals. The underworld. Living in a place where information can be had for a price. Men like that, for a couple of bucks, they'd pull their own mother's fingernails out."

"But they wanted my ID. What's that all about?"

Colonel Olsten frowned. "My thought, too."

"Freddy has more guts than I do."

"No one trusts anyone where he is."

"It's getting spooky around here, Colonel."

"You got it."

That night lying in bed, trying to fall asleep, Zenji knew he would never be the same. The personality of the city was changing, and so was he. One thing was sure: whenever the back of his neck tingled, he would go on full alert.

He shuddered . . . then bolted upright.

"Jeese!"

Without warning, the tingling had sprung up again, crawling all over his skin: what if John Jones *hired* those guys . . . to roll me . . . for my ID? He kept asking if I was military. No one else ever has. What if he got those guys to search me?

But why?

That was the big question, not really the ID itself. *Why* did John Jones want to know if I was military?

It didn't make sense.

One thing he knew—it was only a feeling, but it felt as real as a slap in the face: John Jones was not the American he seemed to be. There was something different about him, something bad.

He was hunting, looking for something.

That thought made Zenji shiver. Maybe Jones was hunting him.

But *why*?

Zenji lay back and put his pillow over his face. "Freddy," he mumbled. "Be careful . . . very, very careful."

20
BENNY SUZUKI

At the post office one day in mid-November, Zenji received instructions to report immediately to G2.

When he got to Olsten's office, the colonel said, "I have an assignment for you, Zenji, one you might find interesting. I want you to get to know someone. We've had eyes on him for a while now, but we need to get closer. I think you can do that for us."

"Not John Jones, I hope."

The colonel frowned. "Mr. Jones is still a mystery to us, but I've got people following up on it. No, this person is a young attorney from Honolulu by the name of Benny Suzuki. He's been working here in Manila as a legal adviser to the Japanese embassy. We want to know what he does, specifically."

Zenji brightened. "From Honolulu?"

The colonel smiled. "That's your ticket in. You two will have something in common."

"So, I just walk in and try to meet him?"

"Exactly. You heard about him from the men at the hotel and you were excited to hear there was someone else in Manila from Hawaii. Be casual. Maybe you're homesick. Nothing more than that. Don't raise suspicion."

"Got it."

"Check in by way of your post office box. Keep me current."

"I will, Colonel." Zenji started to leave, then turned back. "I haven't seen Freddy Kimura around at all. I'm concerned about him."

"Don't worry about Freddy. We've got him on a special assignment at the moment. We just opened up an intelligence language school in San Francisco, and we're having him provide information on the field so new linguists can get a truer picture of what they might be getting into in the Pacific."

"He's in San Francisco?"

The colonel laughed. "No, his office is still the ghetto."

"He can have it."

The next afternoon Zenji stopped by the Japanese embassy on Escolta Street to see Benny Suzuki. No appointment, best to just show up.

He hoped.

Benny's receptionist was appalled that he thought he could just walk in and see someone. "He's very busy," she said in Japanese, hesitant to even let Benny know he had a visitor.

Zenji nodded. "Yes, of course. But I heard he's from Hawaii, like I am. I just wanted to introduce myself. I won't take much of his time."

She eyed him, then huffed and got up. She tapped on a door. "Do you have a moment for an unscheduled visitor?"

Benny came out and gave Zenji an impatient look. "Yes?"

Zenji was momentarily knocked off-balance by how young Benny looked; not even thirty.

He recovered quickly, brightening, trying to look as if he were finally meeting someone he'd been hoping to run into for some time.

He spoke in Japanese. "Mr. Suzuki," he said, extending his hand, "thank you for taking a moment out of your busy schedule. I'm Zenji Watanabe from Honolulu. I'm staying at the Momo hotel and heard from the businessmen there that there was another Hawaiian in town . . . and I just wanted to stop in and say hello."

A smile replaced Benny's impatience. "Honolulu! Great, great." He shook Zenji's hand and switched to English. "It's been a while since I've run into a fellow Hawaiian. Come into my office. What school did you go to?"

He pointed Zenji to a chair.

Zenji sat. "McKinley. Where'd you go?"

"Roosevelt."

"Good school."

"For sure. You go to college?"

Zenji shook his head. "Not yet. Still trying to figure out what I want to do with my life. I'm here mostly because I didn't want to get drafted." That lie had worked well at the Momo.

Benny pulled his chair from behind his desk and sat facing Zenji. "So, tell me how you ended up in Manila."

"Well, I had a job on a ship, but being at sea wasn't that exciting, plus I get seasick. So I jumped ship and found a job at a warehouse. It's something. At least for now."

"And you're staying at the Momo?"

"Just happened on it. I like it there, full of businessmen from Japan." He grinned. "They treat me like a kid brother."

"You speak Japanese well."

"I get along."

"Yeah, me too. Japanese school paid off, huh? That's how I got this job. After law school I couldn't find work back home, so I brought my family to Japan hoping to find something there. They can always use people who speak English. I got a job, but was soon sent here."

"Your family?"

"Wife and son. He's two now. But I'm so busy here I'm lucky to find five minutes to spend with him. He's pretty much growing up without a father, and that's not so good."

Zenji nodded. He felt for the boy. "I know what it's like to grow up without a father. My dad died when I was eight. Accident at work."

Benny winced. "Sorry to hear that."

"Yeah."

After a second of awkward silence, Benny said, "I'm hoping to get some time off." He shook his head. "I'm so swamped it could be a year before that happens."

"You *look* swamped," Zenji said, nodding toward the stacks of paperwork piled on the desk and on a folding table under the window.

Benny grunted.

Since Benny wasn't bringing up U.S.-Japan relations, Zenji decided that he wouldn't, either. Not until Benny did. "If you were back home, you could take your son to the beach."

"Yes, home." Benny looked out the window.

Zenji wondered what he was thinking.

"So," Benny said, regaining focus. "You didn't want to get drafted."

"Yeah, my mother thinks the army is no place for me. She's prob'ly right. Anyway, I wanted to travel and see the world."

Benny nodded slowly, pondering something.

Zenji tried to relax, be careful he didn't say something wrong. You're a civilian, a kid looking to find himself.

"You know," Benny said. "If you have extra time in the evenings, I could use some help . . . and you could make some extra cash. You can see how much I have to do."

"That's a lot of paper, all right."

"Too much for one guy. You could help me out and we could talk about home."

Zenji eyed all the papers. What might they reveal? He didn't want to sound eager. "Well, I don't know . . . I haven't even gone to college yet."

"Don't need college for what I'm thinking. You speak English and Japanese, and that's what matters."

Zenji made a show of mulling it over. But inside he could hardly contain his excitement. Benny's office could be a gold mine of information for G2.

He nodded. "Sure. How can I help?"

Benny grinned, tapping his fingers on his desk. "Did you

know that the U.S. just froze the assets of all Japanese citizens living in the Philippines?"

"Really? Why?" Zenji hadn't heard that news.

"Just happened, and I don't know what caused it. But one thing is sure—I'm going to be flooded with requests, absolutely flooded."

"Requests for what?"

"Asset reports. All Japanese nationals need to file a report with the U.S. High Commissioner's Office. You can assist me by interviewing people and helping them fill out their declaration forms."

Colonel Olsten wasn't going to believe this.

"Do you think war is coming, Benny? I mean, between us and Japan?"

"I sure hope not."

"What will you do if it does?"

Benny looked down. "I don't know."

In a moment, he glanced back up, and Zenji saw the worry in his eyes. "I've got my family here."

Zenji held Benny's gaze until he felt uncomfortable. "Hey . . . uh . . . you sure I don't need college to help you out?"

Benny blinked and took a breath. "Positive."

"Well . . . fine, then," Zenji said. "What do I have to do in the evenings, anyway? I can help you."

THE NERVOUS MAN

Colonel Olsten could hardly contain himself when Zenji told him about Benny Suzuki's invitation. "Do it!" he said, astounded by the unexpected opportunity. "This is brilliant, Zenji! Brilliant!"

"Yes, but it's awkward, in a way."

"What do you mean?"

"Well . . . he's just working for them. It's a job. He couldn't find work in Honolulu. He's not really a *Japan* Japanese. If we got in a fight with Japan, he'd be in a jam. I don't think he'd choose to be on their side."

"Why is that awkward?"

"I wouldn't be able to help him without admitting that I'd also been deceiving him."

Colonel Olsten thought a moment. "Yes, true. Time will

play itself out, I suppose. Let's just hope our diplomats are making progress."

On his first day of working for Benny Suzuki, Zenji learned how to help applicants fill out their asset declaration forms, and for weeks after, that's what he did in the evenings.

He quickly got over his reluctance to question his elders, who graciously understood that he was helping them, not being disrespectful.

There wasn't much to it, really. It was way easier than operating a forklift, and far more interesting than a fake job in a warehouse.

Zenji set himself up in his room at the Momo hotel and offered his services. Benny paid him, but it was free to all Japanese nationals. When word got around about how easy it was to get help with the forms, Zenji received a ton of business, and was soon a kind of star at the Momo.

"Look at you," a businessman said at dinner one night. "At first you were just a kid who jumped ship. Now you're a lawyer."

"Come see me when you get in trouble," Zenji said.

"I like your rates. No charge."

That caused a laugh.

Zenji grinned, and added, "Yeah, but for you I've been thinking about raising my rates."

As he laughed, Zenji felt ill thinking about how deep his betrayal was becoming. It was the ultimate disrespect.

But he had a sworn job to do.

One valuable thing he learned for G2 was that somewhere around half the businessmen in Manila were Japanese military reservists, something Colonel Olsten had suspected and now knew for a fact.

But that wasn't all.

One evening, a reluctant customer showed up at Zenji's hotel room. He looked to be in his fifties and introduced himself as Saburo Hiashi. "I am a Japanese language school principal," he said. "Can you help me with these forms?"

"Of course. Come in. Please."

Zenji led him to the small desk near the only window. A gold-shaded lamp cast warm light over their work space.

Mr. Hiashi sat and placed the forms on the table in front of him. He glanced around Zenji's room, his eyes darting from one spot to another.

He's nervous, Zenji thought. Or maybe shy. No, that couldn't be it. He was a school principal.

Zenji noticed his fingers were thick, and his hands were rougher than one would expect of a principal, as if he were also a gardener or one who worked outside in some way.

"So," Zenji said. "Let's take a look at what we have here, Mr. Hiashi."

Mr. Hiashi pushed the forms closer.

Zenji flipped through the pages, smiling to put the man at ease. He was far more nervous than anyone Zenji had helped so far. Why?

"I'm quite familiar with these forms," Zenji said. "We'll just start at the top."

Mr. Hiashi nodded. "It must be done."

"Yes," Zenji said, amazed at how devoted these men were to following the letter of the law. He understood; it was his culture, too.

Zenji filled in Mr. Hiashi's basic information—who he was, where he lived, how he was employed and for how long.

When they got to a question regarding his military service, Mr. Hiashi fell silent.

Zenji looked up. "The military, Mr. Hiashi. Are you now, or have you ever served?"

"Do I have to answer?"

Zenji sat back and looked across the table. "Well, I guess you could skip it. But it would raise suspicion if you left it unanswered."

An uncomfortably long moment of silence followed before Mr. Hiashi spoke again. "What happens if I have served, but say I haven't?"

Zenji put his pen on the table. "I don't know, Mr. Hiashi. I suspect that would be up to the person reading these forms."

Zenji waited.

There's something important here.

Mr. Hiashi pursed his lips. "I am the ranking officer in the Philippine Japanese Reserve Corps."

Zenji squeezed his hand into a fist under the table as a distraction. He must not show one fragment of the surprise he felt. This was precisely the kind of information Colonel Olsten needed to know.

"I see," he said. He rubbed his chin, as if in thought. "That would make me hesitate, too, Mr. Hiashi."

Mr. Hiashi shifted in his chair. He almost smiled, as if relieved that Zenji was sympathetic. "I trained at the Nakano School for intelligence officers. It was an honor to have been chosen."

"Indeed," Zenji said. "Indeed."

Mr. Hiashi could be a possible source for a lot more information. "Listen," Zenji said. "Why don't we take a chance and say you've never been a part of the military. It's most likely that no one will pursue it further."

Mr. Hiashi nodded once, with authority. "Thank you."

"Well, don't thank me yet. Someone may question it."

"I understand."

Zenji finished with the forms and handed them back. "There you go. Turn them in and forget about it."

Mr. Hiashi stood, bowed curtly, and left.

Zenji closed and locked the door. He sat on his bed to write his report. "With this I might get promoted to general."

He chuckled.

Someone rapped on the door.

Zenji stuffed his report under his pillow and stood up.

It was Tadeo. He looked pale, spooked. "We just heard . . . a ship has arrived from Japan. They're evacuating all Japanese embassy personnel and their families."

"What? When?"

"Immediately."

22

FULL ALERT

The news caused a near panic at the hotel.

Guests poured out of their rooms to stand in line around the two telephones in the lobby, trying to call home and see if anybody knew what was going on.

Nobody knew anything.

The evacuation had not been made public. Tadeo had gotten a call from a friend at the embassy, and that was all they knew.

"Maybe it's just a rumor," Zenji said, mingling among the guests. He should call Benny. He'd know.

"But the ship," Tadeo said. "Why would it be here?"

The next morning Zenji headed off to his fake job. As far as he could tell everything was normal. No one on the streets seemed any different. At the warehouse he asked if anyone knew about an evacuation of Japanese nationals. No one knew anything.

He slipped out the back door and made his way to the harbor. If the ship was there, then what Tadeo had heard from his embassy friend had to be true.

There it was.

A long gray Japanese passenger liner alongside the wharf.

Silent in the still water.

It gave Zenji the creeps.

It won't be long, he thought. When people see crowds at the harbor, and lines of people climbing aboard that ship, Manila will know something is up, something bad.

What had happened to provoke this?

The best he could guess was that U.S.–Japan diplomatic talks had broken down. But that wouldn't necessarily mean war. It would just mean the U.S. and Japan weren't talking.

Right?

Nothing more happened that day, and there was no notification in his mailbox.

And there should have been.

In the deep, dark silence of the night, Zenji's fears ran wild. Small thoughts morphed into Japanese battleships moving silently closer on moonlit seas, heading toward Manila. Zenji imagined the worst of everything, his mind wrestling with all possibilities. If Japan was taking people out, something else was coming in. Something was going to happen in Manila.

Were the Japanese going to invade?

They couldn't! Manila was an American commonwealth!

First thing in the morning, Zenji headed to the post office and checked his box again.

A note.

Come in. Immediately.

I knew it, I knew it, I knew it!

On the way to Fort Santiago, Zenji detoured to the harbor to get another glance at the Japanese ship.

Still there. Loading people.

Zenji read the name—*Nitta Maru*.

He worked his way closer, blending into a growing crowd of curious Filipinos. He absorbed every possible detail to report to Colonel Olsten.

He was about to leave when he glimpsed something that stopped him cold: Benny Suzuki . . . in line with his wife and son. He was going to *Japan*?

Why? He was an American.

Benny wouldn't choose to take sides against his own country. Zenji was sure of it. Maybe he was being forced.

His heart raced. His world was about to fall apart. He could feel it in the air, like electricity.

War!

It was coming.

Zenji stayed at the harbor, watching, and was surprised when after boarding with his wife and son, Benny came back down the gangway. He stood a moment looking at the ship, then headed back into the city, his gaze on the ground.

Get to G2.

Now!

In the colonel's office, Zenji could hardly stand still.

Colonel Olsten was on the phone, talking low. He stuck one finger up. *Just a minute.*

How can he be so calm at such a time?

Colonel Olsten hung up. "You know about the ship?"

"I was just down there. I saw it."

"Tell me everything you know. Everything."

"Benny Suzuki put his family on board . . . but he got back off."

"Interesting. What else?"

Zenji told him about Mr. Hiashi, and the chaos at the hotel when they got word of the evacuation.

The colonel listened with squinting eyes, as if trying to call up a memory. He went to a filing cabinet and searched through the folders in the top drawer. He pulled a photo out of one of them. "This Mr. Hiashi?"

Zenji took it. "Yes. That's him."

The colonel pursed his lips and put the file on his desk.

"Why would Benny Suzuki send his family to Japan? He's an American."

The colonel paced, thinking. "Don't know, but this is my guess. Mr. Suzuki was hired by Japan for his legal skills and his ability to speak two languages. So my guess is that he's simply evacuating his family with those who hired him. What I'm not sure of is whom he would side with in a conflict."

"Us . . . for sure, us."

"Maybe so."

"What's going on?"

Colonel Olsten paused, lost in thought.

"Colonel?"

The colonel looked up. "We've been put on full alert . . . *all* American forces in the Philippines."

Zenji stared at Colonel Olsten.

"You're thinking war, I can see it in your eyes. But there's been no provocation, other than a breakdown in diplomacy, and that could all get ironed out tomorrow."

The colonel leaned back against his desk, rubbing his chin. "Here's what I want you to do. Continue your surveillance at the hotel and in the Japanese community in general. If things deteriorate, and war becomes imminent, it'll happen fast. We and the Filipinos will start rounding up all Japanese nationals in Manila . . . and when we do, I want you to get rounded up with them."

"You mean get arrested?"

"Exactly, but make sure you get arrested by the Filipinos, not us. Stay with the nationals and get every bit of information you possibly can. We need knowledge, so keep your ear to the ground. And don't worry, we'll find a way to get you out when the time is right."

"How will you know where I am?"

"The Filipinos are our allies. We'll know everything they know. Don't worry, I'm not going to leave you hanging."

Zenji stared at him. The colonel had better be right, or he'd end up in a Filipino prison.

23

INCRIMINATING EVIDENCE

At the Momo hotel, worry about the evacuation had died down, mostly because the embassy workers themselves had not been sent away, only their families. So there was a small sense of hope that something would be worked out.

Still, an uneasy feeling remained.

One day a letter arrived at the hotel for Zenji. Tadeo handed it over. "From your family, looks like."

Zenji grabbed it. "Thanks!"

He took it to his room and sat on his bed.

It was from Aiko, the first letter he'd received since he sent her the postcard with his address on it. It had taken weeks to arrive, and it felt like treasure.

He tore the envelope open.

A photograph fell out. He smiled.

Ken and Nami. Ken's eyes were squished closed as Nami licked his face.

He unfolded Aiko's letter, and another letter within it fell out, along with one of Ma's poems.

Slowly, savoring the moment, he opened the other letter. Who was it from? Henry? Ma? Colonel Blake?

Mina.

"Oh, wow," he whispered.

He stared at it a moment, then folded it back up, unread, and set it on the bed beside him. Save it for last.

Read Aiko's first.

Dear Zenji,

How are you doing, so brave way down there in the Philippines? The picture on the postcard you sent looked nice. I didn't think Manila was that big. Even Ma was surprised.

Nothing much is going on here, except that Ken—remember the boy who has Nami? Well, he came by with his mom and brought Nami. Ken's mother asked us to send you this picture. She said to tell you that Nami is doing fine. You can only tell he had that accident because he limps a little. I was so happy to see him again. So was Ma, but she didn't show it while Ken and his ma were here.

Anyway, we all miss you. Henry and I talk about you all the time. We wonder what you're doing. Come home soon. Ma sends you this poem. It's true. We miss you.

And you see that there is another letter in this
one. I wonder what it says. Mina has been to our
house every week since you left. I like her a lot.
She took me to a movie called In the Navy, *starring*
Abbott and Costello. It was funny! Henry says to
tell you to stick with him, whatever that means.

> *Your sister,*
> *Aiko*

Zenji smiled.

Your sister, as if he didn't know.

He felt honored, somehow. It wasn't like Aiko to write letters. He could only picture her buzzing around the neighborhood on her bike, not sitting in the house working on a letter. But then, she was a year older now.

He read Ma's poem next.

> *Daily*
> *We pray*
> *For the safe*
> *Return of our son*
> *And brother, who*
> *We miss*
> *Dearly.*

Zenji felt the pain of sadness in his chest. Boy, did he miss home. "Thanks, Ma," he whispered. He loved her crazy poems. They were comforting, and sometimes just what he needed.

Like now.

He picked up Mina's letter and unfolded it.
Slowly.

Hi, Zenji,

   *It's Mina, the one who made you dance when
you didn't want to. I should say I'm sorry I made
you do that, but I won't because I'm not. If I
hadn't, I would never have gotten to know you and
your very special family. Aiko told me about Nami
and the boy in the picture. Such a beautiful story.
Girls don't meet guys like you every day, and I
hope I get to know you better when you return. I
know I'm being bold, but that's just the way I am,
as you know from Tosh's party. I believe a person
should never deny what she feels in her heart.
What I feel is worry for you and pride in your
courage. I have to trust that you are safe wherever
you are.*

   *I hope saying these things doesn't make you
nervous. I'm just being honest, and at times like
these, with so much uncertainty, I don't want
to hide behind something as foolish as pride or
embarrassment, if that makes sense. No matter
what happens, I want you to know that you will
always have a friend in me.*

   *You will come back to us, Zenji Watanabe. Safe
and sound.*

Yours,
Mina

Zenji held the letter, just staring at it.

Pride in your courage.

His eyes flooded. He was completely overwhelmed to know that people cared for him. He had no idea that such feelings existed within him.

He looked at the photo again, then slipped it into his wallet along with Ma's poem. He would carry them with him always.

He memorized Aiko's and Mina's letters, then tore them to shreds and flushed them down the toilet. They could incriminate him. Both mentioned bravery and courage. Why would someone say that to a civilian?

That night, he slept fitfully.

The next morning Zenji went down for breakfast and found the hotel deserted.

TOWERS OF SMOKE

It was Monday, December 8, 1941.

Zenji couldn't find anyone, not even Tadeo, or cooks in the kitchen.

His heart began to pound. Something was up.

He hurried out, trying his best not to run to the post office for information, anything to tell him what was going on. On the streets, everything seemed normal. The day was peaceful, the streets settling down after the morning rush.

Nothing.

His mailbox was empty.

Huh.

Nothing out of the ordinary was going on at his fake job, either, so he slipped out the back and into the streets.

Minutes later the world as he knew it fell apart.

A newspaper boy down the street began shouting, "Extra! Extra! Read all about it! Japanese attack! *Extra!*"

What!

Zenji ran the two blocks and gasped when he read the headline plastered across the front page of the newspaper in the boy's hand.

PEARL HARBOR BOMBED!

It took a moment for him to understand. Pearl Harbor?

So close to his . . .

No!

No, no, no!

He bought a paper and raced through the story. "This can't be!" The Japanese had bombed Pearl Harbor the day before! Damage was near total. Ships and military aircraft were destroyed. Thousands of men had died. Ships were still burning. Even the oily surface water in the harbor burned.

There was a photograph of smoke stacking into the sky, with crumpled and burning battleships listing precariously below.

How did the Japanese get there?

Did they send troops ashore?

Was his family in danger? Were they injured? Had his house been bombed?

He raced back to the hotel.

This time he found chaos.

Tadeo, the guests, and the staff had all rushed to the Japanese embassy when they'd heard the news, and had just returned. After receiving a phone call that morning, Tadeo had alerted his Japanese guests that their country was at war with the United States. They'd hurried to the embassy to verify the horrifying news.

The businessmen were incredulous, to say the least. Even though many of them had expected a conflict, the reality of what had happened was shocking.

The men were clumped in groups, talking loudly. No one knew what would happen to them, stranded in Manila, an American commonwealth.

Zenji, too, felt the charge of fear, his veins running hot with anxiety. If this was war, did that mean that he was now an enemy to his friends at the hotel?

He ran to his room and jammed things into his duffel in case he had to evacuate. Forget the suitcase. Be ready to get out, fast and light. If his cover was blown and he was found out, he had no idea what would happen. He could never face these men. Never!

Calm down! You won't be exposed.

Except—did John Jones know he was the Bamboo Rat, a spy? But who was John Jones? A nosy American, or a traitor working with the Japanese?

He sat on his bed. Tried to slow down, breathe.

Remember what the colonel said: If you get captured, keep your cover. Stay with the nationals, but only get arrested by the Filipinos.

A siren wailed in the distance. Zenji leaped up and ran to the window. "Oh, jeese!" he gasped.

In the distance, to the north, towers of black smoke billowed into the sky.

He raced back down to the lobby.

Tadeo was trying to get everyone's attention, but no one

was listening. Their voices were a din of panic. He glanced at Zenji, desperate.

Zenji understood, and whistled as loud as he could.

Everyone stopped talking.

Tadeo held up his hands. "Listen! Stay calm, and listen! Clark Field is being bombed, right now. The Japanese are attacking the Americans! The Japanese are attacking Manila!"

Clark Field was only forty miles away! Where he'd seen the black smoke.

Like ants, the men scattered.

Tadeo motioned for Zenji to whistle again.

"Listen!" Tadeo shouted. "Listen! This is important! I've just had a call. The Philippine Constabulary is on its way to this hotel. It has been ordered to evacuate all guests. Every Japanese national in Manila is being removed to the Nippon Club and will be held there until further notice."

Zenji knew the place, a Japanese club for meetings and family sports.

"Pack your essentials now!" Tadeo shouted. "The constabulary is close!"

Men ran to their rooms.

Less than fifteen minutes later, two huge buses and a Philippine military truck ground to a halt in front of the Momo. Troops from the constabulary rushed out to cover the exits.

Zenji looked down from his window. Here it comes. He prayed Colonel Olsten knew what he was doing.

Zenji grabbed his duffel and went downstairs to join the nervous but orderly line of businessmen as they were herded onto one of the buses. Japanese families and more business-men already on the bus sat grimly, watching them board.

Zenji squeezed into a two-man seat with two other guys.

The ride was silent.

Minutes later, the bus grumbled up to the Nippon Club, a huge two-story building with sprawling green lawns and tennis courts. Hundreds of men, women, and children were already there.

The bus hissed to a stop, and emptied, leaving its sullen riders standing with their gear in the sun. No one told them what to do, so they milled around asking each other questions that no one could answer.

Prisoners.

Or at least temporary captives.

Even though he knew he had a way out, Zenji could feel the emptiness that rushed in to fill the space of lost freedom. But he couldn't simply wait for something to happen. You made life happen your way or you let it happen to you.

He could help or be herded like a cow.

He spotted a child, a girl of six or seven, who couldn't stop crying. Her dazed mother had lost interest in consoling her. Zenji knelt before the girl, and his sudden presence momentarily distracted her. He pulled a coin from his pocket, showed it to her, then laid it on top of his hand and magically rolled it over his knuckles.

The girl watched, mesmerized.

Zenji rolled the coin back and forth a few times, then stood and gave it to her. Her mother gazed at the ground, grim. If hope existed, it had gone into hiding.

He glanced around at the other families, scattered in

groups on the grass, their meager belongings in neat clumps around them. Everyone looked to be in shock, talking low, glancing around furtively. He couldn't blame them. He'd feel bewildered, too, if back in Honolulu his family had been uprooted and bused to some new location without knowing why.

The constabulary decided that women and children would shelter inside the club, and the men would remain outside wherever they could find a spot. Zenji spent the next couple of hours helping families find places to settle.

"Hey," he said, breaking up a fight between two boys. To think that Japan had uprooted their safe and secure lives— had started a war, had bombed Pearl Harbor, and now Clark Field, smoke still scarring the sky—it was all unimaginable!

The boys backed off and stared at Zenji.

"It's going to be all right," he said. "We don't have to fight between ourselves. Look, it's like camping. We're going to have a good time."

He refused to believe the friendly Filipinos would be anything but respectful.

"Think about all these people," Zenji said to the boys. "Show them how to be strong, how to work together. I know you can do that."

The boys glanced at each other and nodded.

"Good," Zenji said. "Go help your families set up camp."

Officers of the Philippine Constabulary helped people as best they could. None seemed harsh, though many were suspicious. Japan had just bombed their country.

Zenji lost himself in the crowd.

It wasn't the constabulary that he worried about. It was

the Japanese! What if they had ships nearby and troops came ashore? What if they took the city and discovered that he was working undercover for the U.S. Army . . . a spy in the Japanese community? They'd execute him on the spot.

He crouched under a tree, trying to calm himself.

It could happen.

Be strong.

Breathe.

As soon as his nerves settled, he got up, found his duffel, and took it to his new home—a blanket in the corner of a tennis court.

25

HANDCUFFED

For three days Zenji wandered around the Nippon Club, listening in on conversations, watching for anything unusual. But as far as he could tell, there were no spies among these people. If there were, they were very good ones.

On the fourth day, Zenji was handcuffed and taken away by an officer from the Philippine Constabulary.

"What's this all about?" Zenji asked. "What did I do?"

The Filipino officer did not respond.

Zenji's fear subsided somewhat when he remembered what Colonel Olsten had said: *Make sure you get arrested by the Filipinos, not us.*

One of Zenji's friends from the Momo saw what was going on and hurried over. He followed them out, speaking in Japanese so the officer couldn't understand. "Why don't you tell him you're American? You don't have to be here."

"Safer in here. Outside, they'd take me for ... you know ... somebody who just bombed them."

"Ah. So it is. Smart thinking."

Zenji tried to get the officer to stop a moment. "At least let me say goodbye."

The officer gave Zenji a few seconds.

"Listen," Zenji said to his friend, "please say goodbye to the others for me. Be well, all of you. I hope you get home safely, and soon."

He wished he could do something for them.

The Filipino officer hauled Zenji out to a black car. Another officer stood waiting, and got in the back with Zenji.

The car pulled away, leaving the Nippon Club.

"Did Colonel Olsten send you?"

Neither man answered.

"How about these cuffs? Can you take them off?"

Nothing.

Zenji had to sit leaning forward, the cuffs pinching his wrists behind his back. He tried to relax. Colonel Olsten must have ordered this. Why else would he be here?

Trust.

Trust Colonel Olsten.

He looked out the window as they drove.

Manila was already changing—store windows crisscrossed with tape, sandbags piled into small bunkers on the streets, snarled and tangled traffic slowing the black car's progress to a crawl, herds of people fleeing town, long lines outside of banks. Zenji felt bad for the citizens of Manila, caught in a mess they had no stake in creating.

Fortunately, Japanese troops had not come ashore.

But what about in Honolulu? Had they landed there?

He'd have heard about it, wouldn't he? Wouldn't people be talking about that?

Maybe not.

Too much chaos.

Was his family okay? His neighborhood wasn't that far from Pearl Harbor. Was Henry all right? Where he worked was even closer.

Maybe he was hurt.

Stop! Don't think!

Zenji closed his eyes in relief when the arresting officers turned in to Fort Santiago and not a prison. They cleared the gate and stopped at Colonel Olsten's building. The man in back helped Zenji out and removed the cuffs, still without a word.

An American guard headed out to take charge. "This way," he said.

"Where are we going?"

No answer.

These guys don't see an American, Zenji thought. They see an enemy.

When they entered the G2 office, Colonel Olsten jumped to his feet. "Zenji!" He dismissed the guard and pointed to a chair.

Zenji eased into it, rubbing his wrists.

"Sorry you had to come over in cuffs," Colonel Olsten said, sitting back down. "But it was better for your cover."

"That's all right."

"I got—"

"Colonel, have you heard anything about Honolulu? I'm worried about my family."

Colonel Olsten leaned back. "From what I've heard, the city itself suffered some, but overall it's intact. Most damage was confined to military sites. Your family should be fine."

Zenji looked at his hands. Thank God.

What about Mina? Had she heard about Manila? Was she worried, too? He wished he could get word home.

"Such a tragedy," the colonel said. "It was a complete surprise."

Zenji looked up. "Can I call home, Colonel?"

Colonel Olsten shook his head. "Not possible. Not now, anyway."

Zenji pursed his lips.

"Pearl Harbor and Clark Field weren't the only places they hit. They bombed Hong Kong, Singapore, Thailand, Wake Island, and Guam, as well."

Japan had been bold beyond measure. Beyond imagining. "Colonel— That's crazy. They just smacked a beehive with a stick."

Colonel Olsten sat back. "I'm going to have you work for me here at the fort. There are coded radio intercepts to unravel and a few captured enemy documents to translate. We even have a few POWs already. We need you to interrogate them."

"POWs?"

"Downed pilots."

Zenji stared at the colonel. "Wait. Did you say you want *me* to interrogate them?" He was incredulous. He could translate, but interrogate? "I have no training for that."

"Understood. But at the moment we have few choices. You speak the language, we don't. We'll help you as we can."

The colonel looked Zenji in the eye. "You and Freddy Kimura are all I have here. We need information and will do what we have to do to get it, because it's going to get worse. Guam is in Japanese hands now."

"Is that bad?"

"Very. They're coming here . . . soon . . . and when they do, we won't be able to stop them."

26
SWITCHBLADE

A few days later, Zenji ventured outside the fort. He needed a break, a walk, some fresh air, anything to break the monotony of reading through stacks of paper and listening to jabbering radio transmissions.

Where was Freddy? What did they have him doing?

Zenji stood in the sun and took a deep breath. He'd been living in the barracks, eating in the mess hall, and hadn't been outside the fort for days.

He started walking, just a few blocks. He had only a half hour.

Five minutes. That's all it took before that creepy feeling in his neck kicked in. He glanced around, trying to be inconspicuous.

They were easy to spot.

Two young Filipinos, following him.

Memories of Chinatown flooded his brain, but his experience with the four guys who'd attacked him in the alley made compassion sound ridiculous.

His pursuers closed the distance between them.

Zenji hurried across the street, cutting between honking cars. The two men stayed with him, closing fast.

When Zenji stopped to look into a store window, the men mimicked him. When he moved on, so did they.

Amateurs.

But who were they? What did they want?

For the first time he noticed people glaring at him. This is because I'm Japanese, he thought. Should have stayed inside the fort.

He wasn't paying attention, and soon found himself boxed into a dead-end alley.

He turned back.

The two men stood motionless at the alley's entrance.

"What do you want?"

One guy pulled a switchblade and popped it open. The men started walking into the alley.

Zenji backed up.

"Hey!" someone shouted.

The two guys stopped and looked behind them.

Freddy!

"Back off!" Freddy was holding a .45-caliber pistol, government issue.

The guy folded the knife, his eyes saying, *Next time.*

The two guys backed out of the alley and blended into the foot traffic on the street.

Freddy holstered his pistol.

Zenji breathed deeply. "Man, am I glad to see you!"

Freddy grunted. "They think you're a national."

"Figured that. Let's get out of here."

They headed back to the fort. "Olsten just called me in," Freddy said. "I came looking for you. Some guy told me you were going batty, stuck in that room."

"Yeah, I was. Lucky you came looking."

"I was tailing you and those guys. Practicing."

"Thanks for letting me suffer."

"Those punks were nothing."

"How'd you get the gun?"

"Asked for it. Kind of dangerous where I am. I heard you visited."

"It was ugly."

"Not so bad once you get to know it."

They started back to the fort. "You saved me, Freddy. They would've cut me."

"No problem. What you been doing since last time I saw you?"

"Mostly keeping an eye on some businessmen, but they don't know anything. What about you?"

"Not much. Helping out with a new intelligence program in San Francisco."

"Yeah, heard about that."

"Olsten said Pearl Harbor got it bad, but the rest of Honolulu is okay."

"You're lucky. Maui was spared."

Freddy shook his head. "Nobody was spared, if you think about it. This war will be around awhile."

"Probably. Hey, I ran into another guy from Hawaii. You heard of Benny Suzuki?"

Freddy nodded. "Little bit. On the wrong side, I take it."

"I'm not sure about that. He got a job in Japan and ended up in Manila."

"So you talked with him?"

Zenji told him the story. "And get this—I worked for him. Undercover, of course. He's a good guy."

"With bad timing."

"What's worse is he had to evacuate his wife and kid to Japan when that ship came in. He stayed behind."

"I know," Freddy said. "I think he's a prisoner at Fort McKinley now. If it's the same guy, we took him in with the rest of the embassy staff after the Japanese bombed Clark Field."

"But he's American. How can they do that?"

"Think about it."

Zenji frowned. "They think he's on the wrong team?"

"Bingo."

"We have to get him out, Freddy."

"Never happen."

"But he's innocent."

"Working with the enemy is innocent?"

"Working *for* the enemy, Freddy. There's a difference. Japan wasn't the enemy when he took the job."

Freddy shrugged. "Not my problem."

Zenji would talk to Colonel Olsten. He had to do something. Benny had the same problem he and Freddy did. If the Japanese took Manila they could easily think Benny was a spy, and the worst kind—an American inside their own embassy.

He'd live about five minutes.

UNBEARABLE DISGRACE

At Fort Santiago, Zenji and Freddy worked long hours side by side at metal desks in a cave-like room. Since there was no need for cover, they wore khaki uniforms like any other soldier.

For Zenji, this was a relief. If he were captured he'd be better off as an army clerk than an undercover spy, especially one of Japanese descent. At least, he hoped that would be the case.

One day, six letters from home—all sent on different days, but delivered in a clump—arrived on his desk. Two were from Aiko and Ma, one was from Henry, two from Colonel Blake, and one from Mina.

Only Henry's was written after the Japanese bombed Pearl Harbor.

Little Brother,

It's crazy here right now, and probably just as bad where you are. I can't say much, because, as you may know, every piece of mail that leaves the islands is ▮▮▮▮▮▮▮▮▮▮▮▮. So I'll just say what I can and see what gets through.

First, all the ▮▮▮▮▮ are closed. And we have to ▮▮▮▮▮▮▮▮▮▮▮▮▮▮▮▮ at night. There's a curfew, so no one can stay out late. The ▮▮▮▮▮▮▮▮▮▮▮▮▮▮▮ the place. It's ▮▮▮▮▮▮▮ now. But the worst thing is that all Japanese are ▮▮▮▮▮▮▮▮▮. They think we had something to do with ▮▮▮▮▮▮▮▮; which is nuts.

The day after ▮▮▮▮▮▮ I joined something called the Hawaii Territorial Guard. We were given a ▮▮▮▮▮▮▮▮▮▮▮. Our job was to ▮▮▮▮▮▮▮▮▮▮▮▮▮▮▮▮▮▮▮, and things like that. Just yesterday, they kicked all Japanese guys out, calling us enemy aliens. I want to sign up, but can't. They don't want us. Anyway, what would Ma and Aiko do without my pay? It's crazy.

Someday somebody will feel ▮▮▮▮▮▮▮ having done this to us, but that's how it is here. I hope you are safe.

Write me when you can.

Be brave, brother.

For Pop.

Henry

Enemy aliens?

Zenji wanted to write back. What Henry had written made

his face hot, even what little was left in the letter to be read. But anything he wrote would be censored just like Henry's. It was almost pointless to write at all.

Hi, Ma. Doing fine. Wish I was there, not here.

That kind of thing.

Brainless.

But he did write to let them know he was okay.

One day Colonel Olsten showed up with a new work plan. Freddy would continue with the radio intercepts and captured documents. But for Zenji the colonel had a "change of pace."

He clapped a hand on Zenji's shoulder. "We're going to have you talk to a few tight-lipped men."

Freddy looked at Zenji and wiggled his eyebrows. "Interrogation."

Zenji stared at the colonel. "I—"

"I know, you have no training. We'll give you a few pointers beforehand."

Pointers.

Sweat rolled down Zenji's back as he sat waiting at the interview table in the stuffy, windowless basement room. Concrete floor, metal table with a pitcher of water and two glasses, four chairs, and one door. Above, a single bare bulb.

The pointers were: sound friendly; be relaxed; pour him a glass of water; ask important questions more than once; act like you're on his side, just trying to help.

All useless, because the second a guard brought the first prisoner in, Zenji's mind went blank.

He rubbed his palms on his pants and stood.

Something will come. Relax.

The colonel had said, "Take charge of the room right away. Look and act confident. You're the leader, he's the follower. First impressions are very important."

But Zenji found it difficult just to look at the guy.

He fingered the papers on the table between them.

Colonel Olsten had prepared the questions. Most were easy, like where was the guy from and did he have a family, questions to make him relax and, hopefully, open up.

But there were also questions about missions and the war. "Don't be pushy and shut him down," the colonel had warned. "It will be a fine line you walk."

You can do this.

Zenji looked up.

The prisoner was staring at him. He wasn't bound or shackled, and it surprised Zenji that the guy was so young, only a couple of years older than he was.

"Namae wa?" Zenji asked.

The pilot took a breath as if to speak, but said nothing.

"What is your name," Zenji repeated.

"Hamamoto," the pilot said slowly, having trouble speaking.

Zenji suddenly understood—the man was utterly stupefied to have found a Japanese among the enemy Americans. How could this be? No Japanese would ever side with them.

After a few easy questions, Zenji took a moment to assemble his thoughts. Now for the important questions. He had to do this right.

"You are a pilot?"

A slight nod.

"Your plane was shot down. You bailed out and were captured."

Hamamoto glared at Zenji.

Zenji didn't avert his eyes. "What was your mission?"

Hamamoto turned away. "Kill me," he said, his eyes tearing. "I must die."

Zenji knew that if there were a knife on the table Hamamoto would grab it, not to kill Zenji but to kill himself for the inexcusable shame of having been captured.

Zenji sat back. He completely understood the pain. This was his own mother's creed. *Die before shame.* For this pilot, after losing the plane and being captured, it was better to die.

Zenji studied the man, wondering how far he himself would go to atone for some perceived shame to his family name. Was he this kind of Japanese? Maybe.

"You feel disgraced," Zenji said.

Hamamoto faced Zenji. His eyes were glazed over, as if he'd taken himself out of this world and into another.

It might be impossible to get anything out of him now. He had most likely been irreversibly indoctrinated, and would never reveal even one word of useful information. It was the kind of thinking Zenji had learned at Japanese school as a kid.

"There is no shame in having been captured," Zenji said. "That's only what you have been trained to believe. There is no dishonor here, none. To be taken prisoner is just part of war."

Hamamoto sat staring at the table.

"You must accept that you are a prisoner now. With that

come certain responsibilities. One of those responsibilities is to tell us what you know. There is no disgrace in your honesty. Do you understand?"

Zenji couldn't believe what he'd just said. Where was this coming from? A *responsibility* to confess?

Hamamoto blinked.

Zenji studied him, slowly piecing it together. This pilot had never been trained to deal with interrogation. Capture wasn't considered. One would *never* allow it. He would kill himself first.

And now he was unable to.

Hamamoto seemed to have no idea what to do.

Except, perhaps, to follow Zenji's lead. He sat ramrod straight and stumbled through the questions, obviously trying to hold back the important facts.

"That's all I know," the pilot said.

Zenji didn't believe it, but he nodded. He had one more trick to try, something that would hit Hamamoto in the center of all he believed.

"I will interrogate your companions," Zenji said. "If you're lying to me, I will know, and you will be in a very different situation."

Hamamoto looked down.

"May I remind you of this most important fact," Zenji added. He paused to give his next words their full weight. "There is no honor in dishonesty."

Which was when Hamamoto broke down and gave Zenji all that he'd been holding back.

28

THE ROCK

On December 24, General Douglas MacArthur, commander of U.S. Army Forces in the Far East, ordered G2 to leave Fort Santiago immediately, which sent Colonel Olsten scrambling.

A few days before, the Japanese had landed their main force at Lingayen Gulf, about one hundred miles north of Manila, batting the Filipino reservists aside like bothersome ants. Two days later, they landed another force south of Manila. The Americans were now caught in a giant trap.

Zenji and Freddy spent Christmas cramming important documents into fifty-gallon fuel drums and setting them afire.

"You scared, Freddy?"

"I'd be an idiot if I wasn't."

"What do you think they'd do to us if we got captured?"

"Remember Nanking?"

Zenji looked at Freddy. "We're dead if they discover we're army. We should work on our story."

Freddy grunted as he heaved another box into the fire. "I got a better idea: don't get caught."

Word came down that G2 would evacuate to Corregidor, the tiny rock fortress that stood guard at the entrance to Manila Bay, twenty-six miles away. The island sat in the open sea just a few miles south of the Bataan Peninsula. Zenji had heard Corregidor was full of tunnels built by the army for bombproof storage.

General MacArthur worked around the clock, accumulating supplies and as much ammunition as he could lay his hands on for Corregidor's antiaircraft batteries.

They would need every bit of it.

Just before they left Manila, the last satchel of mail arrived. There was one more letter for Zenji. It was from Aiko. It was short and to the point.

Dear Zenji,

Please write home. Ma is very worried. She sits alone and looks out the window. We are all worried. Did you get my last letter? Are you getting any letters? Maybe you wrote and we haven't gotten it yet. I hope so. But write so we know you're safe. We read that Japan bombed Clark Field and the naval base near you. Are you safe? Write and tell us.

Do it now.
Please.

Aiko

They would get his last letter soon. He hoped.

With the Japanese forcing them to evacuate, it was probably the last letter he'd be able to send for a while.

That night, in early January 1942, along with the hundreds of American troops still left in Manila, Zenji and Freddy boarded an interisland steamer and set out in blackout mode on a zigzag course designed to evade enemy submarines.

"They call Corregidor 'the Rock,'" Zenji said.

He and Freddy stood at the ship's rail, looking back at Manila.

Freddy pointed with his chin toward the blacked-out city. "In a few days that place will be crawling with Japanese troops."

"Spooky," Zenji said.

"What are we going to do with all our prisoners?"

"Who knows? Move them somewhere."

Colonel Olsten appeared beside them, a shadow. "You two just got special orders. General MacArthur has assigned you to be his personal interpreters. You'll be working in his office on Corregidor."

Zenji's jaw dropped. "The general wants *us*?"

"You're the best we have."

Freddy clapped his hand on Zenji's shoulder. "With him we'll be safer. Nobody's going to let anything happen to General MacArthur."

Colonel Olsten agreed. "We'd be in bad shape if something did."

"We'd be in bad shape if a sub got us, too," Zenji said, looking out over the black bay. "Gives me the creeps being this exposed."

"Boom!" Freddy whispered. "We're on the bottom looking up."

Two hours later, the ship docked safely at Corregidor.

As the line of men headed inland, Zenji made out the shadowy shapes of tents and antiaircraft guns.

"Marines from Shanghai," Colonel Olsten said. "They had to evacuate, too. But unlike us, they have weapons." He started up a slope. "I hope you boys like spiders."

"Hate those things," Freddy said.

Which made Zenji wonder: was he still the Bamboo Rat? There might be a few Japanese nationals in a cell who knew about Americans with code names who had been slinking around Manila. If there were, they could soon be released by the invading enemy.

And he'd be hunted.

John Jones came to mind. Creepy as he was, Zenji could not see him as a traitor. He was probably just an American living in the Philippines, maybe even a common criminal.

But he had said he'd lived in Japan for a while.

The guy was a mystery.

They set up in one of the dusty barracks. Zenji found a bunk that wasn't too saggy and shoved his duffel under it, too tired to check for spiders. Anyway, spiders didn't bother him . . . unless, of course, they were black widows . . . or some monster thing they had in the Philippines.

He fell asleep instantly.

The next morning as Zenji and Freddy headed out to a mess tent, a squadron of planes burst over the hills and bore down on them, machine guns blazing.

"Zeros!" someone shouted.

Japanese fighters, followed by three bombers.

Freddy and Zenji hit the dirt.

Zenji covered his head and curled into a ball, making himself as small a target as he could. Bullets spat up dirt inches from his face.

After the first pass, he got up and ran for the trees.

Men scattered for cover like disturbed ants. Marines sprinted toward the antiaircraft emplacements. Some shot into the sky with their rifles, hitting nothing.

A Zero flew low to survey the situation, shot straight up, banked, came back around, and strafed the encampment. A bomber came in after it and dropped a bomb that blew out all the windows on the side of one of the barracks. The blast knocked Zenji off his feet and rang in his ears.

The bomber thundered past, rising, banking to circle back.

Zenji spotted Freddy out in the open firing at the planes with his .45. "Freddy! Hide!"

Freddy sprinted behind the barracks.

The Marines got the big antiaircraft guns up and running, swung them around, and started blasting the sky.

Boom! Boom! Boom!

The Zeros didn't like that and went after them.

Zenji watched, crouched under a tree, witnessing combat for the first time. The antiaircraft batteries pummeled the enemy. A bomber peeled off and plunged toward the sea, trailing smoke. It hit the water and tumbled like a wheel, ending in a great *whoosh* of white water.

All Zenji could do was stay where he was. He had no weapon, and even if he had, what good would it do? He'd never been trained to use one.

Bombs whistled as they fell. Thundering explosions shook the earth. He covered his head, his heart pounding like a hammer.

Minutes later, it was over.

The Zeros flew off with the two remaining bombers, antiaircraft fire chasing them.

When the big guns ceased firing, an eerie silence fell over Corregidor. Fires and clouds of smoke blossomed upward. The smell of exploded ordnance hung in the air.

Zenji crept out into the open . . . and stopped, sick.

He'd never seen a dead man.

Three bodies lay crumpled before him.

29
LAST PLANE OUT

For two months following the Zero attack, Corregidor was peaceful. The damage hadn't been all that bad, but the once beautiful island was now scarred with shredded trees and gaping holes.

As the Japanese closed in on Manila, General MacArthur set up headquarters in Malinta Tunnel, an eight-hundred-foot tube with twenty-five lateral tunnels on the north and south sides. It had been built into Malinta Hill by the Army Corps of Engineers more than ten years before.

General MacArthur didn't like hiding in a tunnel. It went against his grain. But the importance of his mission overrode everything else.

Freddy and Zenji worked for him, though never directly. Their assignment was to try to make sense of intercepted communications, monitor Japanese radio transmissions, and pass on what they found to MacArthur's staff.

Every day Freddy and Zenji examined the huge map on the wall that kept track of U.S. and enemy troop movements. "Look at this," Freddy said one day. "They're cornering General Wainwright."

On the map, Wainwright's troops on the Bataan Peninsula were getting battered. Pins showed the enemy pushing them closer to the ocean every day.

Zenji watched the situation deteriorate. General MacArthur paced. The peninsula was just a few short miles across the bay north of Corregidor. When Zenji and Freddy left the tunnel for fresh air, they could walk to spots where smoke across the water was visible.

"Those poor guys are getting pushed into the sea," Zenji said.

"Be glad you can speak Japanese, or else you might get sent to join them."

"Show me how to shoot first."

"You don't need a gun. You need a tank."

Zenji shuddered, thinking about what must be going on over there. "Don't we have any reinforcements?"

"Nope."

"Amazing how they keep holding on."

Freddy frowned. "They better start looking for a boat."

In March 1942, General MacArthur was ordered to relocate to Australia. The situation in the Pacific had gone from bad to worse.

MacArthur pulled General Wainwright out of Bataan to

take his place on Corregidor, leaving another general, Edward King, to fight on in the peninsula. Zenji felt bad for General King. What courage he and his men must have.

Freddy and Zenji watched as General MacArthur and his staff fled Corregidor in a torpedo-armed attack craft called a PT boat.

"He didn't look happy to leave," Freddy said.

"Would you?"

"No. Feel like I was running away."

"You heard his speech. He said he'd return. I believe it."

"So do I."

Zenji cleaned his glasses. They headed back to their quarters silently.

In early April, U.S. forces on the peninsula were very close to being overrun. The news was all over the tunnel, and men were short on patience, snapping at this and that.

"We're next," Freddy said. "They'll be coming to take Corregidor. . . . Glad I still got my pistol."

Zenji looked at Freddy blankly, at a loss for words.

"They're closing in, brother," Freddy said. "You got any civilian clothes with you?"

Zenji had left pretty much all he had in Manila when they evacuated. Now he had only what he could grab from the supply room: two pairs of khaki pants, and shirts with no insignias.

"I'm in the same boat," Freddy said. "Only saved one civilian shirt."

They agreed that they were probably just days from getting their heads chopped off. They joked about it, but deep inside, Zenji was paralyzed with fear.

Freddy said, "See if someone will issue you a .45. You need *something*."

"No, Freddy. I'm telling you. They come ashore, ditch that thing."

"Pssh."

"I'm serious. If they catch you with a weapon they'll shoot you. They won't think twice. It would infuriate them to see a Japanese fight against other Japanese."

"We'll see."

And they would, because General King and his forces were quickly overcome and captured. The Bataan Peninsula was now entirely in Japanese hands.

Corregidor was next.

Within a week, the enemy had set up artillery on the southern tip of Bataan and began lobbing ordnance over the water to pummel Corregidor's battlements.

Colonel Olsten pulled Zenji aside. "I've got General Wainwright's permission to send you and Freddy out of here to join General MacArthur at his headquarters in Australia. We may not be able to hold out. If we're overrun, you two . . ."

He let that hang.

"I understand," Zenji said. "But what about you?"

"Don't worry about me. I'll make out. Listen. We have only one chance to get you two out of here. In a few days a small aircraft will take you to Mindanao. From there, you'll transfer to a B-17 and head on to Australia. Be ready."

"Yes."

Zenji and Freddy packed their duffels and lived out of them until the order came to head to the airfield. Zenji knew he'd miss the colonel. But even so, huge relief washed over him.

A couple of days later, something else popped into his head.

Benny!

Was he still imprisoned at McKinley with the Japanese embassy staff? Or had the prisoners been moved out, too? Maybe by now he was in a Filipino prison. Had the Japanese moved into Manila yet?

Alarms went off in his brain: Benny's in the same danger as me. If the Japanese take Manila and release the embassy staff—find an American among them—they might take him for a spy and execute him. His family in Japan would live in disgrace, maybe even on the streets!

Alone.

Zenji was gripped by the memory of Benny's wife and small son climbing aboard the passenger liner.

He knew that Benny would never choose to side with Japan. He was loyal, a Hawaiian.

Zenji had to help him. Benny's family needed him. Zenji could fend for himself along with everyone else on Corregidor.

"I want to give my seat to Benny Suzuki, the guy you had me spy on at the Japanese embassy."

"What? This is your only—"

"He's an American just like me, Colonel. The Japanese could call him a spy and execute him. He's in the same position that I am. They won't trust him."

Colonel Olsten frowned, thinking.

"His wife and son are in Japan. What happens to them if Benny is executed as a spy?"

Colonel Olsten pursed his lips.

"Please. I want to stay. I belong here."

The colonel sighed. "He's in McKinley. I'll have him released immediately and sent here. As for you . . . well, you need weapons practice."

"Yes."

The boat carrying a confused Benny Suzuki to Corregidor arrived late the next night. The plane to Mindanao was taking off at midnight. In the dark it would be a risky flight, but in daylight—suicide.

Zenji and Freddy waited at the dock.

"I can't believe you're giving up your seat," Freddy said.

"He's one of us, Freddy. And he's got a family."

"Still, he was with *them*."

Zenji shook his head. "Twist of fate. Unlucky. Doesn't matter. I gotta help him."

"You're nuts. You're also a good guy, Zenji, and braver than me. . . . I'm proud to know you."

Zenji glanced at Freddy, then away. "I'm proud to know you, too, wise guy."

They shook hands, hanging on a bit longer than usual.

"Banzai," Freddy said, and Zenji laughed.

They were dressed as civilians. The last thing Zenji wanted Benny to know was that he'd been tricked, that Zenji was in the military and had spied on the Japanese embassy. Benny had trusted him. Zenji could explain everything later. But not now.

Benny got off the boat carrying a small bag. He was thin now, older. When he spotted Zenji his face lit up.

"What are *you* doing here? How'd you get out of prison? Didn't you get caught up with the guys at the Momo hotel?"

"Long story," Zenji said, turning to Freddy. "Meet another Hawaii guy, Freddy Kimura."

Benny and Freddy shook.

"Let's go," Zenji said. "Not much time."

"Time for what?" Benny asked. "I don't even know why I'm here."

"You're going somewhere safe."

Benny grabbed Zenji's arm. "Another prison?"

"No! You're an American. We're getting you out."

"We?"

"I meant the army. There's a small plane with one last seat. Yours. Come on!"

They started to run.

"Where are we flying to?"

"You'll see. Go! We're late."

They ran over to an idling jeep that zoomed off into the night.

"I'm staying here," Zenji shouted over the jeep's roar. "The army needs me to translate."

"But you're a civilian."

"You're a civilian, too, and you have a family. That's why I begged them to get you out."

Benny looked at him, stunned.

They made the airstrip in time. Freddy shook Zenji's hand. "Catch you on Maui sometime."

"Save me and Benny some mangoes."

"I'm sorry to leave you, partner. You've been a good rat." Freddy smiled and ran to the waiting plane.

Benny clutched Zenji's hand. "Thank you! *Thank* you! I hope . . . I'll see you back home."

"Me too, Benny, me too."

"Zenji!" Freddy shouted from the plane. "Good luck!"

Zenji waved.

Benny clapped his hand on Zenji's shoulder. "I'll never forget this, my friend!"

Two hours after the plane took off, the island was pounded by heavy artillery from Japanese ships offshore.

Along with General Wainwright, his staff, Colonel Olsten, and the rest of G2, Zenji retreated into the depths of Malinta Tunnel. Even there they could hear the explosions and feel the earth shake.

The lights flickered and went out.

They crouched in the dark, whispering, waiting.

"You should have taken that plane," Colonel Olsten said.

"I'll be fine."

"You're going to be questioned, son, and you must— *must*—stick with your cover. If they take you for a U.S. spy, it's over."

Zenji gulped, his mouth dry. "I'm a . . . I'm a civilian working for the army. That's all."

"Stick with that. No matter what."

"Yes."

"No matter *what*!"

THEY WANT THE TUNNELS

On May 1, 1942, the battle for Corregidor began with relentless aerial bombardments, followed by crushing artillery barrages from the sea. Zenji now understood what it meant when someone said death was knocking at your door.

Japanese artillery accuracy was highly enhanced by spotters in observation balloons high above Bataan, only two miles away. From there they could clearly see the American targets and relay that information to their gunners.

The only real safety lay inside Malinta Tunnel, but just a fraction of Corregidor's eleven-thousand-man garrison could fit in, mostly army headquarters and the hospital.

At one point, Japanese artillery rained down twelve 240-millimeter shells per minute for five hours, eating away at the island's concrete defenses.

Just before midnight on May 5, a brutal barrage came in from the sea, and while U.S. troops dug deep into their foxholes, eight hundred enemy soldiers came ashore near the airstrip on the tail end of the island.

To the east, another eight hundred found their way inland.

The sound of the fighting reverberated through the tunnel. Zenji crouched near General Wainwright, his hands over his head, hoping the bunker wouldn't fail and cave in on them.

At five-thirty the next morning news came: an additional nine hundred Japanese troops had landed with heavy vehicles. At nine-thirty, three Japanese tanks began to systematically pulverize marine battlements, and move steadily beyond.

"They're coming here!" someone shouted from the far end of the tunnel. "They want the tunnels!"

General Wainwright went white.

Zenji, too. If those tanks came inside and started blasting, no one would survive.

Zenji's whole body began to shake. *Fear will never control me.* That was so easy to say back home, where he couldn't imagine terror such as this. Henry, you have no idea. There were over a thousand wounded men in here, and every one was helpless.

As the sound of Japanese tanks blasting away at the hillside grew louder, General Wainwright turned to his staff. "Enough! I will not allow one more man to die in this hopeless battle. We can't hold out. We have to cut our losses now, before more men die."

Zenji waited, hardly breathing, as General Wainwright

conferred with General Lewis Beebe, his chief of staff. "I . . . I hope to God I'm making the right decision."

After a moment of painful silence, General Wainwright said, "General Beebe, prepare a statement of surrender."

Immediately, men scattered, General Beebe barking orders.

"Watanabe!" General Wainwright snapped.

Zenji ran up. "Here!"

"Come with me. We need you to translate our . . ."

He could not say the word.

"General Beebe will broadcast it in English first, then you will repeat it in Japanese."

"Y-yes, but—"

"Follow me," the general said, subdued.

Hopelessness was a feeling Zenji had never known before. Even when Pop died he still felt hope—because of Ma, Aiko, Henry. But now, to give up. Surrender . . . he couldn't grasp it.

"That's an order!" General Wainwright snapped.

Outside the tunnel, the tanks clanked closer.

General Beebe stared at the microphone for several seconds before he spoke. The muscles in his jaw rippled.

"Go ahead," General Wainwright said softly.

This is killing them, Zenji thought.

General Beebe began.

"Message for General Homma, message for General Homma."

The radio transmission would be picked up in Cabcaben, Bataan, where General Masaharu Homma was thought to be headquartered.

General Beebe identified himself, saying he and the United States military on the island of Corregidor wished to surrender.

"At twelve hundred hours we will raise a white flag and cease all military actions against Japan. At that time I will send two members of my staff to Cabcaben on a boat, also flying a white flag. There, they will meet with General Homma and arrange a formal surrender. Once that has been completed, I will meet personally with General Homma at a site designated by him."

Zenji's breath caught when General Beebe turned to him. "Repeat that in Japanese."

On his first word, Zenji stuttered.

Think!

Say it perfectly.

He breathed deeply. Settle down.

Zenji read the message.

The response was immediate.

It was transmitted into English by a loud, arrogant, low-level officer. "General Homma will not meet with staff members, only General Wainwright himself. Not only will you surrender Corregidor but also all American and Philippine troops in the region. There will be no other option but this."

The transmission ended.

General Beebe turned to General Wainwright.

The general thought a long moment before responding. "Tell General Homma that I cannot surrender on the terms put forth without first meeting the general in person."

The next response came from someone other than the low-level officer. "General Homma will agree to meet General Wainwright at Cabcaben."

The communication ended.

Outside, the sound of tanks ground to a halt, and though battle could still be heard beyond, an eerie quiet settled over the men inside the tunnel.

General Wainwright turned to Zenji. "You'll come with me."

Zenji nearly choked. "To Cabcaben?"

"I will need you there."

BORN IN AMERICA

General Wainwright, his staff of ten, and Zenji set out in a small boat for the short journey to the Bataan peninsula.

The ocean was calm. Zenji wore his civilian khaki uniform, no insignias. He was just employed as a translator.

Breathe.

Be calm. Think like a priest. Remain in control.

Your story *must* stick.

Be brave. For Pop.

If you only knew, Henry. If you only knew.

Within five minutes of leaving shore, a Japanese fighter swooped down for a closer look, then circled once and followed in wide arcs above.

"Stay on course," General Wainwright ordered the boat pilot. "If they think we're making a run for anywhere but Cabcaben, that fighter will sink us."

"They'd love that," someone spat.

Zenji knew that if the guy who'd said that had had a weapon, he would fire at the plane. Many of the general's troops, and some on his staff, wanted to fight to the last standing man. Like the Japanese pilot Zenji had interrogated, the humiliation of surrender and being taken prisoner was unacceptable.

But the general was finished with death. His goal now was to preserve life.

Zenji watched the circling fighter, gleaming in the sun. All around was the most peaceful sea, the shiny glint floating in a cloudless sky above . . . yet behind them lay the monstrosity of death and destruction on the Rock. And ahead . . . terrifying uncertainty.

None of it seemed real.

"I have no reason to believe General Homma will be anything less than honorable," General Wainwright said.

The tang of fear, like copper, tingled on Zenji's tongue.

The hum of the engine filled the silence as a boat landing came into view. "Here we go," someone muttered.

A detachment of armed troops waited onshore.

Zenji realized he was about to come face to face with the armed enemy for the first time. He tried to relax his clenched jaw. Be cool, remember your story.

The boat eased up to the dock.

The boat pilot tossed a rope to a man on the pier, who pulled the hull close and threw a hitch over a cleat.

The second the boat was secured a Japanese sergeant major began spitting orders unintelligible to all but Zenji.

"What's he saying?" General Wainwright asked.

Zenji started to translate. "Sir, he—"

"Don't call me sir," General Wainwright said through gritted teeth.

Zenji winced. *Careful!*

"He wants us to debark, line up in single file on the dock, and identify ourselves. Now."

"Do as he says, men."

Facing the Americans with twenty armed, grim soldiers lined up behind him, the sergeant major began at one end of the line. *"Namae to kaikyu-wa?"*

"He wants to know your name and rank," Zenji called down to the man facing the sergeant major.

The sergeant major snapped his head toward Zenji and put up a hand to stop the guy from answering.

Zenji choked.

The sergeant major slowly swaggered down the line to Zenji.

Zenji's hands began to tremble.

The sergeant major came within inches of Zenji's face. Zenji could see right into the man's brain.

He swallowed.

Contempt flared in the sergeant major's eyes.

And some confusion.

"Filipino?" the sergeant major asked in Japanese.

"No, sir. American."

The sergeant major glanced down the line of men from Corregidor. "You are Japanese?"

"Nisei. Born in America."

The sergeant major glared, then smashed his fist into Zenji's face.

Zenji staggered, his glasses flying. Electrical explosions

blossomed in his eyes. His hands flew to his face and came away bloody. His left eye began to swell.

"That's quite unnecessary!" General Wainwright barked.

The sergeant major glared at Zenji, now bent over with blood dripping into his hands.

In that instant, Zenji was no longer afraid. He was enraged. Humiliated. No matter what these animals did to him he would never confess his military status. He would die first.

Slowly, he straightened and met the sergeant major's eyes.

"Why are you in the American military?"

"I am not in the military. I'm a civilian translator."

"You are lying."

"I am not."

The sergeant major spat on Zenji's shirt.

Zenji ignored it, picked up his glasses, put them back on. The frames were bent, but he could see. He regained his place in line, his gaze away from the sergeant major.

So much for what he'd learned about Japan in Japanese school. There was no honor in this. No *meiyo*.

"We don't need you," the sergeant major said to Zenji. "We have our own translators." He called to three of his men. "You, you, and you! Take this traitor away."

Two of the men grabbed Zenji by his arms, but they averted their eyes, shamed by the sergeant major's brutality. Did he treat them the same way?

There is hope, Zenji thought, surprised.

General Wainwright and his staff went to meet with General Homma, leaving Zenji with his guards on the dock.

Zenji's face hurt like fire. He spotted a wooden box and sat. The guards did not object.

174

He removed his damaged glasses and tried to reshape them. He cleaned the dusty lenses with his shirt and wiped blood from a cut on his face.

And waited.

General Wainwright's meeting took a little over an hour. As he and his staff returned, the guards made Zenji stand.

"They treat you all right?" the general asked.

"Fine. We just waited." This time he remembered not to add *sir*.

"How's that eye?"

"I'll live. Thank you."

General Wainwright grunted and stepped down onto the boat. When everyone was aboard, a young Japanese lieutenant jumped in after them.

He smiled at Zenji.

Zenji nodded.

"Don't worry," the lieutenant said in English. "I'm just going with you to help with the surrender."

Zenji tried not to react. He sat near the bow and turned his cut and bruised cheek, swelling nose, and aching eye into the cool breeze. His shirt was covered with blood.

The lieutenant sat next to him. "Why are you, a Japanese, in the American army?"

Zenji kept his gaze on the sea. "I'm not in the army. I'm just an employee. American. Born in Honolulu."

"What do you do?"

"Help with translations."

"Like what?"

"Whatever they give me."

"That's all?"

Zenji turned to look at him. "That's all."

The lieutenant was quiet a moment. Then, "You might be interested to know that your friends are concerned about you."

Zenji cocked his head. "My friends?"

"From the Momo hotel."

Jeese! He knows? "Oh. Yeah . . . I stayed there for a while."

The lieutenant nodded, waited a minute, then added, "Oh, and your other friends wonder about you, too."

Zenji gave him a questioning look.

"You know," the lieutenant said. "The pilots you interrogated. I guess you did a little more than translate, huh?"

Zenji strained to hide his shock. The prisoners had been liberated.

I'm dead.

32

HIGH-STEPPING INTIMIDATION

If Zenji hadn't vowed not to give in, he would be suffering the worst fear of his life.

Instead, he squinted at the lieutenant. "I have no idea what you're talking about. I stayed at the Momo, but I'm not an interrogator."

The lieutenant stared at Zenji. "You underestimate me."

Zenji shrugged and turned away, praying that the accusation was only a ploy to get him to confess. The pilots he'd interrogated could certainly identify him. But they weren't here. How could this lieutenant know for sure that Zenji was the one who'd interrogated them?

It didn't matter anyway. It was their word against his. Zenji had his story and nothing about it was going to change.

The lieutenant smiled and looked out at the sea.

To keep his mind from wandering into dangerous territory, Zenji turned his thoughts to something good. Safe. Far
away.

Ma.

He checked—the lieutenant wasn't looking. He removed
the photo and Ma's poem from his wallet. Looking at the
photo of Ken and Nami, he thought, first thing when I get
home I'll visit them.

He read Ma's poem and looked out over the smooth sea.

No matter where he was, she would be watching over him.

But even with his vow, fear stirred deep inside. If he stumbled, he would die. No . . . it would be worse than death . . .
torture . . . *then* death. They would be merciless.

He, too, might beg to die.

On the morning of May 7, 1942, Zenji, General Wainwright,
his staff and officers were lined up inside Malinta Tunnel
with their backs to the wall, waiting for the arrival of General Homma. The official surrender. Zenji's skin prickled
with tension.

A hushed whisper.

A cough, a mumble.

"Keep it down!" General Wainwright snapped.

Silence filled the cool interior, a giant coffin.

Zenji, on the general's right, could sense the man's pro-
found dignity. He honored the terrible position the general
found himself in, waiting for the inevitable, where he would
surrender his command and the ceremonial pearl-handled
pistol.

Yet even now, General Wainwright, like Colonel Olsten,
worried about Zenji.

"Keep the lowest possible profile," he whispered. "I will demand that they treat you as a civilian."

Zenji nodded. "Thank you. I'll do my best."

"We're going to get through this."

Zenji looked him in the eye, hoping that was true. He nodded.

"There are rules in war," the general added.

Right. Like punching someone in the face after they've surrendered. Zenji could only imagine what the general was thinking. He wanted to say how sorry he was, that he understood that there'd been nothing more the general could have done—except die; that it was agony to surrender.

But the general had chosen life for his men.

They stood, waiting.

An hour passed.

Tick-tick-tick.

Part of the humiliation.

Make them wait and wonder and sweat and fear. Break them down like the pitiful dogs they are.

Sounds of men on the move began to echo through the tunnel.

"Stand tall," the general said to his men. "Don't show them that they have frightened or intimidated you. They want to see your fear. That's their pleasure. Keep your heads held high at all times and never provoke them by looking them in the eye."

Boots.

Many boots. Boots with metal taps on them. Marching in unison, making as much noise as possible.

Closer.

Louder.

Zenji tried to still his hands, hating how they always shook when fear struck.

With terrifying precision the Thirty-Seventh Infantry Battalion marched into view—high-stepping in unison, arms swinging, taps thundering!

Each Japanese soldier wore a cap with strange flaps that hung over the ears, making the men appear even more sinister.

"Good God!" someone gasped.

Zenji squeezed his hands into fists. A terrible weakness sucked at his legs. He had to concentrate to stand and not faint.

He swayed, growing dizzy.

No! They're just men. They're trying to intimidate us. It's just noise. Ceremony. Be strong. Do *not* fail.

The battalion tramped in as one perfect unit.

On and on they came, two hundred strong, at least.

Once the commanding officer stood abreast of General Wainwright, he raised a hand. The battalion halted in absolute precision and turned to face the Americans.

Silence blossomed and filled the tunnel.

Zenji nearly stopped breathing.

It was not General Homma who faced General Wainwright, but a mere lieutenant. Another devastating humiliation.

Saying nothing, and contemptuously looking away from the general, the lieutenant held out his hand.

General Wainwright, who towered over the lieutenant, slowly, and with incredible grace, drew the pearl-handled pistol from its holster and handed it over, grip first.

Zenji's eyes filled with tears. He could not stop them.

The lieutenant grabbed the pistol and carelessly handed it back to a sergeant. He turned away from General Wainwright and, smirking, walked down the line of Americans with his sergeant. At the end, the sergeant removed a folded note from his pocket and handed it to the lieutenant.

The lieutenant opened it, and looked back down the line. "Watanabe! Step forward."

33

KEMPEITAI

Inside, Zenji staggered.

Step forward.

He closed his eyes, breathed, and broke rank.

The lieutenant pinned his gaze on Zenji and strolled toward him, hands clasped behind his back.

Zenji steeled himself.

It was as if he were in a dream, watching it all through his smudgy glasses. He saw his death—a public beheading. A disgrace to his race.

The lieutenant stopped and stood so close that Zenji could smell the stink of old sweat and gun oil. The entire regiment stood at perfect attention, not one eye wandering their way.

The lieutenant looked into Zenji's eyes.

At the lieutenant's slightest nod, the sergeant grabbed Zenji by his shirt and yanked him forward.

Zenji stumbled, but kept his head high. *Never show fear. Be brave, little brother. For Pop. Be like him.*

A smile touched the lieutenant's face. He turned to his sergeant. *"Tsurete ike!"* Take him away!

The sergeant shoved Zenji toward an office.

Zenji knew what he was in for when he saw the three men with high black leather boots and white armbands with red print.

Kempeitai.

Japanese military police.

Zenji kept his head up. He would accept his bitter fate without cowardice or remorse.

At least, that was what he hoped.

Stick to your story, no matter what.

He could do this. He had to.

The sergeant pushed him into the office and stood against the wall, expressionless.

My *file!* Zenji thought. Back in Manila, had it been burned? Or had the Japanese found it? Is that what this was about?

Stop!

He tried to clear his mind. Fear and worry helped nothing. They were not real. They were mental constructions. Nothing else.

One Kempeitai forced him into a chair.

Another came forward, a commander.

Zenji looked at the floor.

"You are Japanese," the commander said.

"American Japanese."

The commander considered that. "In the service of the Americans?"

"They hired me." He had to admit that. He'd been captured with the army. If he were only a civilian, why had he been on Corregidor?

Be respectful. He looked up.

The commander pulled a chair close and sat facing him, drumming his fingers on his thighs. "What is your rank?"

"I have no rank, sir. I am a civilian. They needed translators and pressed me to help them . . . before the war started."

"Hmm."

"I'm from Hawaii, sir. I had a job on a boat to Manila. When I got here I decided to stay. That's when I was hired to translate."

"I see."

The commander crossed his arms, curious and amused. He waved his hand. "You will tell us the truth soon enough. Would you like a cigarette?"

"No, sir. I don't smoke."

Just two guys talking.

The commander nodded to the sergeant against the wall.

The blank-faced sergeant strutted over and leaned in close, looking into Zenji's eyes. His fist shot out.

The blow nearly crushed Zenji's windpipe.

He toppled over and hit the floor. He rolled to his knees and grabbed his throat, unable to breathe.

With his knee, the sergeant smashed Zenji's nose and mouth, splitting his lip. Blood poured onto the floor.

Zenji rolled over. The pain was electrifying. He gasped for air.

The sergeant stood over him. "You bow, dog! You show respect!"

It felt as if he'd been hit in the face with a baseball bat.

He pushed himself up on his hands and knees, gulping air, coughing, drooling blood.

The sergeant shoved him over, and Zenji curled up on his side.

The commander lit his cigarette, stood, shook the match, and dropped it on the floor near Zenji.

He left the room.

The sergeant and two Kempeitai dragged Zenji to another office, shoved him onto a chair, and closed the door.

Zenji could feel his upper lip swelling.

A Kempeitai colonel took over. "What is your rank?"

"I have . . . no . . . rank," Zenji croaked, throat on fire. "Civilian."

"Why would a civilian be found here, working with the Americans?"

"I was hired . . . to translate. That's all. I am not military. They hired me before the war."

"Why did you agree to help them?"

"I felt a sense of obligation to the country that has treated me and my family well. To do otherwise would . . . be disrespectful."

The colonel nodded.

"I have no military skills," Zenji added. He could hardly breathe. Pain swelled in his chest.

The colonel paused. Then, "What was your citizenship before the war?"

"American. Born in Honolulu."

Actually, until his mother had legally registered him as an American at the Japanese Consulate in Honolulu, Zenji had

185

held dual citizenship. The fact that he was registered gave him some small comfort. It was supposed to protect him.

"Your parents are Japanese, therefore you are Japanese, and as such you have acted disgracefully against your own people."

Zenji looked down.

"You have been shamefully captured. Did you not consider suicide as an alternative?"

Zenji looked up.

Suicide?

It was how the colonel himself would have dealt with imminent capture. It was deeply Japanese.

"Yes, I considered that," Zenji lied. "But you see, sir . . . I left home without my widowed mother's permission. She objected to my leaving home . . . and I made her life hard. Now I am honor bound to reverse all the pain I have caused her. Committing suicide would only make it worse for her. Therefore . . . I disregarded that option."

The colonel looked at him. "It is very important to honor your parents."

"Yes."

"Did you know that your friends at the Nippon Club are worried about you?"

"No, sir."

"Oh, but you did. You were told on the boat."

Zenji looked down. Everyone knew all about him. He had to be very, very careful.

"Does the name Bamboo Rat mean anything to you?"

Zenji's heart stopped, then slammed in his ears so loud he felt his face flush. A gasp rose; he held it down.

Breathe.

"Nothing . . . sir. What does it mean?"

The colonel smiled. "I think you know exactly what it means."

He motioned to the other interrogator. They left.

Only the sergeant remained with Zenji.

It was over. He was done, caught. They must have captured a G2 operative and tortured the code name out of him.

But did they know the Bamboo Rat was *him*?

Maybe not.

"You will wish you had chosen the honorable alternative," the sergeant said, escorting Zenji outside to join hundreds of American and Filipino captives in gathering the dead and digging shallow graves.

34

THE GUNSHOT

Two days later, Zenji was in the hospital wing of Malinta Tunnel. His lip was healing well enough, as was his throat. He'd been lucky, the medic had said. His windpipe might easily have been crushed and he could have suffocated.

He was on his way out of the infirmary when a Japanese platoon marched in. Zenji froze when he saw who was with them.

John Jones.

He slipped behind a file cabinet.

Jones with the Japanese? A captive?

Captain Thomson, a doctor, had been at his desk when the troops came in. He stood and faced the lieutenant in charge. "What do you want?"

The lieutenant glanced around the room.

Zenji shrank into the shadows.

The lieutenant jerked his head toward Jones. *"Kokowa darega sikitteiruka kike."*

Jones stepped forward. "He wants to know who's in charge here."

Zenji stiffened. Is he *working* for the enemy?

Captain Thomson glared at Jones. "Who are you?"

"Never mind who I am. Who's in charge?"

"I am."

Jones turned toward the lieutenant and nodded at Captain Thomson. *"Konohito."*

"Zenin tsureteike. Samonaito zenin utsuzo."

Jones turned back to Captain Thomson. "He wants everyone out of here. Now. Evacuate. If you don't leave immediately, you will be shot."

The captain's jaw dropped. "Are you serious?"

"Don't fool with him, Captain. Do as he says."

Captain Thomson looked from Jones to the lieutenant.

"Koitsuwo utsu jyunbi wo shiro!" the lieutenant snapped.

Every rifle came up and aimed at Captain Thomson.

"Captain Thomson," Jones said. "For the safety of all, let's try this again. Make no mistake, you are to do exactly as I say. Are we clear?"

Captain Thomson looked hard at Jones.

"Are we *clear*?"

The captain glanced at the armed troops and nodded, slowly.

Jones said, "Good. Get everyone out of here, and out of every bed in this wing."

"Our sick and wounded? You can't," Captain Thomson said, incredulous. "This is our infirmary."

"*Was* your infirmary," Jones said. "Get your patients out and make room for Japanese wounded. If you don't, you will be executed."

Even from the shadows, Zenji could see the captain's eyes burn.

"Here's what you tell that arrogant fool you work for," Captain Thomson said. "We're not going anywhere. The men in my beds are too sick to move. Tell him to take a hike, and you, too, traitor."

Jones's eyes bulged as he turned to the lieutenant. *"Dete-ikimasen."*

The lieutenant shouted, *"Koitsuwo sotoni tsureteitte ko-rose!"*

Zenji gasped.

Shoot him?

Two men lurched toward the captain.

"No!" Zenji stepped forward.

Jones turned and squinted. "Well, well, well. The moment I saw you in Manila I knew you were military. You're one of the spies I was looking for. Of course." He shrugged. "Hey, I would've lied, too."

"I'm not a spy, I'm a civilian who was hired like you as a translator. Only I work for the right side."

"The losing side."

Jones jerked his head for the two men to take the captain away.

They prodded Captain Thomson with their rifles. *"Ugoke! Ugoke!"* Move! Move!

When the captain refused, one soldier hit him in the neck
with the butt of his rifle.

The captain fell to his knees.

They yanked him up and dragged him outside.

A single gunshot echoed through the tunnel.

35
SICK SHOW

The execution of Captain Thomson stunned Zenji for days. It was heartbreaking. He felt deep sadness and raging hatred. The captain had been a good man. Zenji had been beaten up, dragged, humiliated, spat upon, and shamed. But until now, *nothing* had enticed him to kill.

The only solace he could find was in his memories: his family. And Mina.

You will always have a friend in me.

In the quiet corners of his mind, he read that letter over and over.

You will always have . . .

After three weeks in the sweltering warehouse, Japanese ships arrived to remove all Filipino and American POWs to Manila.

Zenji had expected more interrogations, but nothing happened. And he hadn't seen John Jones again. If he had, he would have strangled him. He now knew that he could kill a man.

The lieutenant who'd had Captain Thomson shot scowled at the line of POWs waiting to be shipped off. His men began separating the POWs into Americans and Filipinos.

The Americans outnumbered the Filipinos two to one, yet the Filipinos were herded onto two of the three ships, and the Americans were crammed onto the smallest.

"You!" the sergeant called to Zenji. He pointed to the Filipino ships. "*Susume!*" Move!

Zenji shuffled aboard with the Filipinos. Was this another way of playing with his head?

A half hour later, he stood at the rail watching Corregidor shrink away, the only American on the ship. The Filipino prisoners and Japanese guards left him alone. He liked it that way. No chance of saying the wrong thing to the wrong person.

Where was General Wainwright? Zenji hadn't seen him in days. Had he been treated well?

Midway between the twenty-six miles to Manila, a squad of guards began herding the Filipinos into small groups, then stole everything of value, laughing and showing each other their treasures.

The Filipinos did not resist, standing with blank, unreadable faces. Why did war give men permission to live like vicious dogs fighting over dump scraps?

One Filipino did not want to give up something he wore on a chain around his neck and got a rifle butt slammed into his gut. He fell to his knees and the guard ripped the chain off with a quick jerk, then kicked him.

If that guard was ever caught on the streets of Manila by one of his victims, he would be dead in a minute.

As the ship approached Manila, the two transports carrying the Filipinos disembarked dockside, but the one with the Americans powered down and sat out in the bay.

Japanese troops ordered Zenji and the Filipino prisoners to line up on the shore, facing the water. Silently, they stood looking out at the American soldiers crammed on the transport's deck.

Zenji flinched when a rifle shot cracked over the water.

The Americans scrambled, climbing over the rail, jumping into the water, raking the surface, struggling toward shore until finally they could touch bottom and slog to safety.

Some couldn't swim, and had to be held afloat by others.

Slowly, every American staggered ashore.

Zenji turned away from the sick show. Why would they do this?

He could only conclude that it was meant to teach the Filipinos the futility of challenging the Japanese. Even the Americans crawled at their feet.

The Filipinos watched without visible emotion. They knew the game.

Once ashore, the American POWs were ordered to march in columns to Bilibid Prison.

A Japanese guard jerked Zenji out of line. *"Omae!"* Come!

Zenji followed the guard back aboard the ship he'd come in on.

A sergeant major waited for him. "We have other plans for you, Watanabe. I'm wondering, do you imagine yourself a man of strength?"

"What do you mean?"

The sergeant major chuckled.

Zenji was alone with a handful of irritable guards.

There were no other prisoners on board.

As night fell, city lights twinkled on the water, and the guards roamed the deck, antsy to be on shore. They glared at Zenji, who sat resting against a steel wall.

He was glad they were missing a night on the town with their stolen money.

He closed his eyes and leaned his head back, remembering Manila. The Momo hotel. The Japanese businessmen. Long walks through the city and along the shoreline. Green parks and colorful gardens.

The Pearl of the Orient.

He thought back to Honolulu and Colonel Blake as they'd looked up at the first star to appear that evening. *Another night in paradise,* the colonel had said.

Paradise.

Zenji looked up. That one bright star was easy to find.

Ma could be looking at it. Right now.

When tomorrow starts without you here . . .

She'd written that note for me, even when she was angry.

He saw Aiko, sitting on the porch.

And Ken with Nami, out for a walk with his mom and dad.

And Mina, teaching him to dance, bringing him a mango pie.

Henry, Tosh.

They could all be looking at the same star.

Zenji rubbed his face. I am here, not there!

He glanced over at the guards, now squatting together, talking low. Just men. Just guys. They'd probably been working in some factory a year ago.

He spent the night on the cold deck.

Early the next morning as the crew readied the ship for departure, a man approached. He looked like a businessman, enjoying a crisp new morning.

He smiled. "Sleep well?"

"Well as I could . . . on steel."

"Luxury. When I was a foot soldier I slept in a mosquito-infested stink-water mudhole. I'll take nice clean steel any day."

Zenji grunted.

The man looked back toward the city. "Nice place, Manila. You like it?"

"I like it fine." *But it was better before you came.*

"Would you like to know where you're going . . . Watanabe?"

Zenji's palms began to sweat. Something bad was about to happen. He shook his head.

"First we're going to drop some men off on Corregidor."

"I'm going back to Corregidor?"

The man grinned.

"Not you. You're going somewhere special."

THE REMAINS OF A NIGHTMARE

After Corregidor, the ship sailed north toward Bataan. To Cabcaben, Zenji thought, fingering his glasses. The frames were still crooked, but they worked.

His escort now was a hard-faced corporal. He looked like a stick of dynamite ready to go off.

Dread weighed heavier the closer they got to the peninsula. What was this *special* place he was going to? And why only him?

When the dock at Cabcaben came into sight, Zenji shuddered. The Bataan Peninsula was a place of death and agony. More than seventy-five thousand Americans and Filipinos had been captured when General King and his men were overcome. What had happened to them?

Once off the boat, the corporal shoved Zenji into the back of a small troop truck.

As the truck drove off, dust rolled in from the dirt road. Zenji pulled his shirt up over his nose.

What he could see out the back was grim—rusting hulks of broken tanks and trucks, artillery, discarded rifles, torn and crushed boxes of supplies, helmets, backpacks.

The remains of a nightmare.

Zenji closed his eyes.

See something good.

Eating fresh papaya on the porch.

The sun splattering tree shadows over the yard.

Aiko, laughing on her bike.

His house, his family.

Mina, in his house with the mango pie.

He always seemed to go home when he needed comfort. He smiled, his eyes still closed. Ma had suffered, but she was strong. When Pop died, she mourned and did what she had to do to keep the family going. Zenji hoped he, too, would find what it took to keep going.

After hours of grinding and lurching, the truck pulled up and stopped. Zenji covered his head until the dust settled.

There were only two things he knew for sure: one, he was deep into enemy territory, and two, he was in as much trouble as he'd ever been in his life.

Why bring him so far? They could have thrown him in prison in Manila with everyone else.

A young lieutenant appeared. "Out!"

Zenji's legs nearly buckled as he tried to stand after sitting so long.

"Welcome to our hotel."

An old military fort.

The lieutenant moved Zenji along. "We have a fine room waiting for you."

A six-by-six-foot windowless cell.

For a week Zenji survived on leftovers provided by guards who were kind enough to spit a few morsels back onto their plates and shove them into his cell.

At first he couldn't even look at the half-chewed food on the greasy metal plates. But by the end of the third day, he ate.

On the eighth day two men came for him.

They took him to a room with a small window high on one wall. The smell was obscene, a mixture of urine, vomit, and decay.

A single metal chair sat in the center of a scarred wood floor with round holes bored into it. Above, a rafter ran the length of the ceiling, and from it hung a rope.

Zenji's stomach lurched as the guards forced him down onto the chair. They backed off and stood along the wall, faces blank.

Why were there holes in the floor?

And what were the dark stains marring the wood around his chair?

A silent half hour passed before a man walked in, casually. All the time in the world. He wore the white armband of the Kempeitai, and his smile said he'd been looking forward to this moment.

"I am Colonel Nakamichi. You and I are going to get to know each other."

Let me be strong.

The colonel slowly walked around Zenji. "What is your rank in the American army?"

"I have no rank. I am a civilian."

Colonel Nakamichi stopped behind Zenji.

He leaned close and whispered, "I have heard that you Americans believe in a place that burns with unending fire. Is this true?"

Zenji said nothing.

"I see." The colonel roared with laughter. "And so shall you."

That was the end of the interview. Nakamichi wanted Zenji to think about this place of fire. He knew how the mind created stories more terrifying than reality.

A guard dragged Zenji back to his cell and left him to think about what would happen to him when they returned.

Alone at night, Zenji filled his head with images of terror.

Just as Nakamichi had planned.

37

TREASON

Two months passed before they came for him again.

During that time, Zenji was moved to a twelve-by-twelve-foot cell with five Japanese soldiers whose only crime was that of having been captured by the Americans.

This disgrace was costing them between five years and life in prison.

Zenji felt bad for them. He was grateful that they were quiet and left him alone. He knew they glanced at him from time to time, but he never once caught them doing it.

His bed was a short straw mat on the floor. His warmth, one thin blanket. The *benjo,* the common toilet, was a round hole cut in a plank of wood over a trench. Water flowed down the trench from time to time to wash the stink and waste away.

There was also a small cold-water faucet for everything from drinking to bathing to laundry. It could have been worse.

Outside the safety of his cell, the prison was filled with rapists, murderers, and deserters. Zenji was thankful beyond measure that he hadn't been thrown in with them.

His cellmates didn't bother him, but they made him stay in the corner, where rats crept in while they slept. All night long, Zenji twitched awake as the rodents scurried past.

Morning and evening, the six men filed out to the cook shack and stood in a long silent line with their wooden bowls. Zenji gobbled down the slop, usually white rice topped with ground hot pepper, and a bowl of watery vegetable soup.

One night, back in his cell with his food, Zenji paused and looked at his meal. He imagined it was a steaming bowl of udon, the comforting noodle soup Ma made.

What were the black balls mixed in with the rice? He moved into a spot of light and squinted.

He pointed them out to the men in his cell. One guy picked one out with his chopsticks. The small black ball was attached to a long white tube. *"Mushi."*

Worms!

Instantly, Zenji's stomach knotted.

But still . . . he had to eat.

He tried to pick every putrid worm out. Hopeless. Worm guts had been cooked into the rice. He had two options: toss his food and starve, or cringe and eat.

He ate.

* * *

When they came for him again, he'd been left alone so long he'd forgotten about the colonel.

As the guards dragged him away, his cellmates cowered, wishing they were invisible, praying that they would not be next.

Zenji was taken to the same room. He sat in the same chair and looked at the same holes and stains on the scarred wood floor.

The guards stood outside as two Kempeitai took positions against the wall.

Minutes later, Nakamichi entered, and for a few moments, paced without speaking.

Trying to make me nervous, Zenji thought.

The colonel stopped, and facing away from Zenji, asked, "Have you enjoyed our hospitality?"

Zenji snorted in surprise. Hospitality? Almost funny.

Almost.

The colonel turned.

Zenji looked at a small smear of mud on the toe of one of Nakamichi's shiny boots.

Not as perfect as he thinks he is.

The colonel kicked Zenji's foot. "I have some news." He looked concerned, almost fatherly. "You are in grave danger." He paused. "You have been charged with treason."

"Treason! How can you do that? I'm an *American*."

Colonel Nakamichi opened his hands. "You have interrogated Japanese soldiers for the Americans?"

"They *hired* me. I'm a civilian who speaks both languages. That's all."

"You are not a civilian."

"I *am* a civilian."

"So . . . your code name is the Bamboo Rat."

Zenji looked Nakamichi in the eye. "A strange name. Bamboo Rat. No, that's not me. Why would I have a code name? I'm a civilian."

The colonel sighed. "When you lie, I can do nothing . . . except . . ."

Zenji's mind raced. They had good spies in Manila. But they don't know who I am. They're fishing.

The colonel raised his eyebrows. "Tell me the truth, and . . . maybe then I can save you."

"You can't charge me with treason. I'm not a Japanese citizen. I am an American *civilian*!"

The colonel turned to a guard. *"Isuwo mottekoi!"* Get me a chair!

The guard brought in a comfortable armchair. The colonel sat and pulled out a pack of cigarettes. He shook one out, lit it, and sat smoking.

Zenji's fear rose and fell like a wild sea. He began to sweat. Bamboo Rat was coming up too often. They were trying to connect pieces of information. A feeling like slithering snakes prickled over his skin.

I am a civilian, I am a civilian. There is no other story.

The colonel blew a smoke ring. "Let's start again. What is your name?"

"Watanabe."

"You are Japanese."

"American Japanese."

"Your blood is Japanese."

"American Japanese blood. Born in Honolulu."

"What is your military rank?"

"I have no rank. I am a civilian."

"Where do you live . . . Watanabe?"

"Honolulu."

"The Americans have mistreated you there?"

"No."

"Do you miss Japan?"

"I've never been to Japan."

Colonel Nakamichi stood and crushed the cigarette under his boot. "Are you not ashamed of that? Are you not humiliated to be on the side of the Americans, and not on the side of your family's blood?"

"I am not ashamed or humiliated."

"You speak perfect Japanese. Why?"

"It's the language of my parents. I learned from them."

The colonel shouted in his face. "You are *Japanese*! Yet you fight with the enemy. You are a *disgrace!*"

Zenji clenched his jaw.

Colonel Nakamichi jerked his chin toward the two Kempeitai.

"*Ro-pu!*"

38

THE ROPE

One man left, and two returned.

Zenji kept his gaze on the floor, seeing only their boots and the coiled rope in one of the men's hand. They closed the door.

The man began to uncoil the rope. The other pair of boots stopped in front of Zenji. "Well, would you lookie here."

English?

Zenji looked up . . . and felt sick.

"No English!" Colonel Nakamichi snapped.

John Jones continued in Japanese. "Why do I always find you in some kind of trouble, Watanabe?"

Zenji turned away.

Colonel Nakamichi looked at Zenji. "You have met this man?"

Zenji didn't answer.

The colonel sat back. "It doesn't matter." He nodded to Jones. "Tell me what you know."

"He's military," Jones snapped. "In the Malinta Tunnel I saw him in uniform. He's U.S. Army."

Colonel Nakamichi turned to Zenji. "What do you say to that?"

Zenji pressed his lips tight. One day he would destroy John Jones.

"We had to leave Manila quickly," Zenji mumbled. "I had no change of clothes. I borrowed a uniform. No insignias."

"*Naine,*" Jones said. Not likely.

Zenji glared at him.

The colonel drummed his fingers on the armrest. "*Ashiga tsukanaiyouni musubi agero!*" Bind him! Raise him off his feet!

The two Kempeitai yanked Zenji off the chair. One tied his hands behind his back. The other tossed the rope up and over the rafter.

They're going to hang me!

Still, he would not struggle. He would not beg, or confess. He would *never* be the coward that the murderer Jones was. They'd have to hang him first.

Once the rope was over the rafter, the Kempeitai ripped off Zenji's shirt and strung the rope under his arms, circling his back. They yanked him to his feet and pulled on the rope until he stood on his toes. Then higher, until his feet swung.

The pain in his shoulders made Zenji gasp.

"What is your rank?" the colonel asked calmly.

Tears of pain welled in Zenji's eyes.

Jones stepped back. "Just tell him and end it."

The colonel lurched out of his chair. "Your rank!"

"I . . . have . . . no . . . rank."

"Nugase!" Strip him!

The colonel's reaction felt good. It gave Zenji the power he needed. Nakamichi was losing it because he knew nothing. Zenji was winning.

The Kempeitai stripped Zenji.

He hung naked.

The colonel lit another cigarette and slowly blew the smoke up into Zenji's face.

"One more time. Your *rank*?"

"No . . . rank," Zenji managed. His shoulders felt as if they were about to separate from his body.

The colonel sucked on the cigarette, turning the tip red. He reached out and pressed the glowing embers into Zenji's armpit.

"Ahhh!" Zenji yelped.

He stared through tears into the colonel's eyes as the colonel burned him again, and again.

"Your rank."

Never!

The colonel tossed the pack of cigarettes to the two Kempeitai. They lit up.

Jones watched as they burned Zenji all over his body in the most painful places.

I am not here, Zenji dreamed.

An old soul, very strong.

There was a light, a glow, somewhere in his mind. On the other end of the most excruciating pain, Zenji found himself in an oddly bearable place.

Alive and not alive.

In this place he thought of an ocean, blue and clean.

His vision blurred, and began to fail.

Hurt beyond hurt, he floated in a dark cave at the edge of the sea, caught in an agonizing surge that pounded soundlessly.

Rage and not rage.

"Your rank."

Here and not here.

"You *will* tell me!"

For a second, Zenji saw a small dog, gasping. Refusing to die. In that moment he knew he would live through this torment.

Nakamichi's face contorted. "Traitor to your country! You will *die*! Tell me your rank and I will save you."

". . . Civilian."

I will survive, and I will hunt you down. I will not stop until I find you. You and Jones. I will kill you both.

The colonel raised his hand.

How many more burns?

A hundred? Two hundred?

What did it matter?

Zenji closed his eyes.

Were his arms still attached to his body?

The colonel waved a hand. "Let him down. We continue later."

Zenji squinted through watery eyes. The colonel was a blur, leaving the room as Zenji slumped to the floor.

39

POISONOUS SOUP

They dragged him back to his cell and dumped him. Zenji lay on the oily floor for over an hour before managing to crawl to his corner. His arms worked. Still attached.

His cellmates ignored him, and seemed to be afraid of him.

But Zenji wanted to be left alone.

That night, lying in the dark and staring at the small window high on the wall, he could see a star.

Its clean light against the black sky, more beautiful than any sight he'd ever seen. It was alone, as he was alone, and that filled him with wonder. Even in pain there was still wonder.

He was alive.

Tears filled his eyes. "Ma," he whispered. "I'm here."

* * *

Days passed.

He lay in his corner for hours, until his bladder finally forced him to move. His burns raged, most of them infected.

He needed bandages, ointment, disinfectant. The burns had turned yellow with pus. The only way to clean them was with water from the faucet in his cell, and that water was questionable.

His coarse prison pants rubbed like sandpaper and made the infections too painful to walk. Once, he removed his clothing and shuffled around naked, but the guards forced him to put his clothes back on. When he asked to go to the prison infirmary, they said no.

When he slept, his clothing stuck to his wounds. In the morning he had to peel the fabric away, making it impossible for the wounds to heal.

Zenji's spirits soared when the guards announced that a fifty-gallon drum of clean hot water for the prisoners to bathe in would be placed on the prison grounds. He could almost feel the soothing water wash away the filth. He would heal!

More than two hundred fifty prisoners filed out to sit cross-legged in orderly rows facing the steaming drum of clean water.

But all two hundred fifty prisoners would bathe in the same water. The tub would not be refilled or even reheated. How could this be? The last man would get oily, frigid scum.

Zenji and his cellmates ended up in the front row. He'd be one of the first! He thanked the universe.

But they were all given numbers on small squares of paper—the order of a man's bath. Each would be allowed one minute in the tub.

Zenji stared at his.

212.

He waited over three hours, and when his turn came, the water frothed with oily brown and yellow bubbles. Zenji backed away. That poisonous soup would be worse than lying in rat droppings. It could kill him.

A guard snapped and shoved him back toward the drum. *"Kono kitanai mizuni haitte sono kitanai karadawo arae!"* Get in. Clean your disgusting body!

Yes, his body was disgusting. But the water was worse.

"Haire!" Go!

Zenji sank into the cold scum.

He waited his full minute, absolutely still.

The next day his wounds raged. Zenji begged the guards to let him go to the prison infirmary.

This time they let him.

The young medic gave a quick glance at Zenji's burns. "What is this? How did this happen?"

"I was burned with cigarettes during interrogation. The burns got infected. I have nothing to clean them with."

"Interrogation?"

"More like torture."

"Do you expect me to believe a Japanese officer would do *this*?"

"Yes, that's what happened."

The medic slammed Zenji against the wall. "You *lie*! That would never happen! You are diseased and are trying to blame us for your condition."

"No, sir, I—"

The medic shoved him again. "Get out!"

40
WATERBOARD

Two weeks later, Zenji was back in the interrogation room. With careful washing several times a day, his wounds had slowly improved.

What if they strung him up again? Burned the *burns*? The thought made him feel sick.

Colonel Nakamichi sat in his wicker chair, legs crossed. "Good to see you again, Watanabe."

Zenji managed a slight nod. Maybe courtesy would work better.

"Would you like some water?"

"I'm fine . . . sir."

The colonel nodded. "Have you remembered your American military rank?"

"Sir, I have no rank. I am an American civilian. I jumped ship and—"

The colonel raised a hand. He sighed and nodded to the three guards. Not Kempeitai. Specialists? Brought in to break him?

He braced himself.

Two guards lifted him off the chair and tied his wrists together in front. They flung the rope over the beam and raised his arms over his head.

Zenji's shoulders still ached. He gritted his teeth, waiting for them to jerk him off the ground.

Instead, they came at him with fists.

Whomp!

In the gut.

Air burst out of Zenji with a sickening gasp. His glasses flew.

Whomp! Whomp!

The force of the blows was unbelievable. Hitting him in the gut, face, kidneys, and ears.

Zenji's eyes swelled, his broken nose and shattered lips bled. He remained conscious, but only enough to wish he could die.

"Yamero!"

The guards stopped and stood back.

Nakamichi uncrossed his legs.

Zenji hung limp.

The colonel sighed. "One last time, Watanabe. What is your military rank?"

Zenji said nothing.

The colonel stared at him. "Unfortunate, and so unnecessary. You can end it all right now with one answer."

"Civilian."

"Ho-su mottekoi!" the colonel snapped. Get the hose!

A guard left and returned with a hose. He tossed one end of it to another guard, who opened the window and dropped the hose outside.

The third guard cut Zenji down, dragged him over to a plank and tied him onto it, then stuck a block of wood under one end so that Zenji's feet were higher than his head.

The guard called to someone outside.

The hose came alive as water gushed through it. Now Zenji understood why there were holes in the floor.

The colonel nodded and the guard stuck the hose in Zenji's mouth.

Water pulsed in. Zenji tried to spit it out, but it filled his throat. He gagged, couldn't breathe. Water filled his stomach, backed up, refilled his mouth, poured out. Zenji was drowning.

Today he would die.

"Mou ii!" the colonel commanded.

The guard pulled the hose out and tipped Zenji to the side. Zenji was coughing, heaving, spitting up water.

They lifted the plank and stood him upright to face the colonel.

Zenji's eyes rolled back into his head.

Nakamichi slapped his face until Zenji refocused. "Either you are telling the truth, or you are very stupid."

Zenji felt no urge to answer.

Nakamichi stared at him.

Zenji looked back.

Finally, the colonel nodded, as if in some strange approval. *"Rouya ni tsurete kaere."* Take him back to his cell.

A guard jammed Zenji's bent glasses back onto his face and dragged him away.

He was never interrogated again.

Months later—he wasn't sure *what* month—he was taken to the prison director's office in handcuffs. His burns had turned into shiny scars that would stay with him until his last day on earth.

The director nodded for the guard to remove Zenji's cuffs.

Zenji stood, wanting badly to rub his wrists. *Don't show that they hurt you.*

The director motioned toward a neat stack of clothing on a table. "Put those on after you bathe."

Clean clothes!

"Go on," the director said.

Hesitantly, Zenji picked them up and raised them to his face to breathe the clean deep into his lungs. He'd lived in filth for so long he knew he was holding something precious.

He looked up, confused.

"Be dressed and ready to leave in one hour."

"Leave?"

But the prison director had turned away.

The interview was over.

COLONEL FUJIMOTO

Later that day, clean and in his new civilian clothes, Zenji was handcuffed and taken away from the prison. He was accompanied by a military driver and a guide named Manabu. Neither man said a word.

Zenji's cuffs didn't bother him. He was spellbound, seeing life outside the mud-brown prison for the first time in months—people, colors, ponds, grasslands, weedy fields, bumpy roads, shacks with corrugated iron roofs, rickety corrals, water buffalo, people of all ages on rusty old bicycles. Free, ordinary life in the midst of war.

Amazing.

But freedom had nothing to do with him. Was he headed to some new kind of torture? If so, why dress him up?

His destination, he soon discovered, was Japanese Fourteenth Army headquarters in Manila.

Manabu got out and walked around the car, surveying the area. The driver's eyes followed the guide in the rearview mirror.

"What's he looking for?" Zenji asked.

The driver ignored him.

Manabu opened Zenji's door.

Zenji slid out and stood in the sun. It felt so good to be back in Manila, even this way. He almost felt free.

"Don't get your hopes up," he mumbled to himself in English.

Manabu snapped, *"Omaewa hanasuna!"* You are not to speak!

Zenji nodded. He'd keep quiet from here to Timbuktu if it would keep him out of prison.

Manabu took Zenji's elbow and pressed him toward the building. They made their way to an office on the third floor, the handcuffs drawing curious glances.

Workers looked up from their desks as Zenji and Manabu walked in. Zenji made note: Nine men, two women. Two exits. No guards. The Bamboo Rat was still alive.

"Susume!" Move!

Manabu shoved Zenji past the gaping staff.

A Japanese colonel stood when they walked into his office. Zenji almost laughed. The colonel was around Zenji's size, but his desk was the size of a Ping-Pong table.

Manabu snapped to attention. "Colonel Fujimoto."

Colonel Fujimoto answered with a lazy salute.

Manabu placed the keys to Zenji's handcuffs on the colonel's desk and vanished.

The colonel looked Zenji over, acting visibly annoyed by the intrusion. Zenji knew it was a ploy to establish superiority. He'd seen enough of this tactic to expect it.

The colonel came out from behind his desk and examined Zenji from every angle.

"How old are you?"

Zenji hesitated. "Uh, eighteen . . . sir." He'd forgotten his birthday.

"You don't know?"

"I lost track of time . . . in prison." What month was it anyway? "What's the date, sir?"

"February 1943."

He'd been in prison almost a year.

"You are American?"

"Yes, sir. Born in Honolulu."

Colonel Fujimoto grunted. "What's your rank?"

Nice try. "I have no rank, sir. I am a civilian."

"Uhnn. What is a civilian doing with the American military?"

"They hired me to translate for them."

Even more ridiculous than the colonel's monstrous desk was the way he wore his pants, halfway up his chest.

But the colonel held all the cards.

"You were charged with treason," Colonel Fujimoto said. "You should have been executed."

Zenji said nothing. It was an argument he couldn't win.

"Fortunately for you, we are not a violent people. We are often forgiving, and in your case it seems those who have interrogated you believe your story. Therefore, all charges have been dropped."

Zenji blinked. "What?"

Colonel Fujimoto gazed out the window, his hands clasped behind his back. "Now that you have been exonerated, would you like to join the Japanese army?"

"Uh, no, sir. I'm an American. Civilian."

The colonel said nothing.

Zenji squirmed. Careful! Sound more grateful. You are at his mercy. His decisions are your only options. "I lack the temperament and military skills that you have, Colonel. I would not make a good soldier."

Colonel Fujimoto turned. "You will work for me, then."

Zenji was speechless. No prison?

The colonel squinted, as if expecting some reaction.

"Work, sir?"

"Colonel Nakamichi is a personal friend of mine. It seems you have convinced him that you are an unfortunate civilian, forced to serve the American military. On his assessment, I believe you can be trusted to work for me."

"The colonel said *that*?"

After burning half my body with cigarettes and trying to drown me?

"He is a firm man, but fair. He was looking for a spy. He thought it was you."

"Me? A spy? That's crazy . . . uh, sir."

"Indeed."

"When do I start?"

"Right now."

The colonel grabbed the keys off his desk and removed Zenji's handcuffs. "You will be my personal interpreter."

"But only for civilian matters, right?" He tried his best to sound grateful. "Uh . . . I would be honored to be your interpreter, sir. However, I can't commit treason against my own country and bring irreversible shame upon my family."

That took the colonel by surprise. "Shame? You are Japanese."

"Yes, sir, but *American* Japanese. I cannot betray my country, nor can I shame my family. Surely you can understand that."

The colonel nodded gravely.

Zenji pressed his lips tight. He should not have been so forceful.

"Very well," Colonel Fujimoto said. "You will do menial tasks in this office and also work at my residence as my houseboy. I can also use you to deal with the Filipinos in Manila. And here in this office"—he nodded toward a mimeograph machine—"you can run that thing . . . and make my tea."

Zenji couldn't believe it. Working in the midst of the enemy? The Bamboo Rat is still alive. Eats the roots, kills the plant.

He almost laughed.

"Thank you, sir, for this fine opportunity. I will do my best, sir."

For the first time, Zenji allowed himself to think about something he'd assumed impossible: escape. Could he find a way?

But where would he go?

The island belonged to the Japanese.

Colonel Fujimoto went to the door and nodded to a man in the staff room. "Sergeant, call my driver. Take this man to my quarters and have my staff acquaint him with the janitor's closet."

HOUSEBOY

The colonel's chauffeur eased the black limousine up to a commandeered mansion on the outskirts of Manila.

Ho! Zenji thought. These guys steal big!

The grim-faced chauffeur opened the back door and stood aside as Zenji and Colonel Fujimoto's sergeant got out.

"The chauffeur isn't too happy," the sergeant said with a chuckle as they walked up the steps.

"He doesn't seem to like that I'm here."

"Correct. The colonel already has a houseboy, a cook, and that chauffeur. All Taiwanese. They're territorial."

"Maybe you could tell him it wasn't my idea."

The sergeant laughed. It lifted Zenji's spirits to know that some Japanese military weren't so serious.

Inside, the rooms were spacious, immaculate. "The staff

223

occupies the lower level," the sergeant said. "The second floor is Colonel Fujimoto's."

Zenji whistled, low. His whole house in Honolulu could fit into the kitchen.

"Follow me."

The sergeant introduced Zenji to the cook and the houseboy. They nodded sourly. Zenji wondered if they got paid. Or had they been forced to work?

"What are my duties?" Zenji asked the sergeant.

The sergeant nodded to the scowling houseboy. "Ting will show you."

"I'm sure he will."

Zenji learned his duties by trial and error. The Taiwanese took great pleasure in Zenji's clumsy attempts at serving the colonel. And they made him keep the house spit-shine clean. "You no clean good, I whip you," Ting said.

So at least one of them spoke some English.

"I'm an excellent cleaner," Zenji said. "I'll keep this place spick-and-span."

"What?"

"Spotless. I clean um good."

"You bettah."

For a bed, Zenji got a mattress in a large closet near the laundry room. The closet was about the size of his former cell, and he had it all to himself. It was dry and clean, with sweet-smelling blankets. Sleeping on the mattress was like sleeping on a cloud. And the wholesome food was unbelievably delicious. Zenji took every bite with enormous gratitude. Sometimes he would just hold a slice of fresh bread and stare at it.

Except for silent meals with the others, Zenji kept to himself.

Weeks turned into months. Some days he stayed at the residence and cleaned. Other days Fujimoto took him to the office.

After a while, the colonel started giving Zenji captured American documents to translate. Most had no value—supply sheets, inventory lists, and other documents low on the list to be destroyed before the Japanese moved into Manila.

But one particular communication startled Zenji, not because it was important, but because it had just come in, and it was dated: July 7, 1943. His birthday.

Ho! I'm nineteen!

Happy birthday, me. The last one he remembered he was eating watermelon in his yard with his family. Or was he? It jolted him to not know for sure. Was the watermelon the birthday before that? It even took him a moment to remember what everyone looked like.

His heart sank. It all seemed so long ago.

And now he was emptying wastebaskets.

But at least peeking into those wastebaskets kept his mind from wandering to sad places.

Once a secretary snapped at him. "What are you looking at? This is not for your eyes! If you look again I will report you to Colonel Fujimoto!"

"Sorry, sorry." Zenji bowed deeply.

Careless.

He couldn't get any useful information. Too many people kept their eyes on him. And what would he do with it, anyway?

When the Taiwanese learned that he'd been an American prisoner of war, their contempt deepened. He was lower than they.

Ting began ordering Zenji to perform all the work he himself was supposed to do.

Zenji didn't mind, because he could explore every inch of the colonel's bedroom. If there was important information anywhere in the house, he'd find it.

The problem was, Ting watched Zenji tirelessly.

"Hey!" Ting shouted when he caught Zenji running his hand between the colonel's mattress and box spring. "Whatchoo doing? Looking for girlie magazine? Go out dis room!"

Zenji raised his hands in surrender. "Just making the bed."

"Go! Out!"

"Sure thing, *hanakuso*-brain," Zenji muttered. *Booger-brain* fit Ting perfectly.

"What that mean?"

"It means, you da boss."

"You right, American dog."

Zenji soon gave up searching. He had no hope of contact, no post office box, no G2. But he didn't stop thinking about escape. If he could ever work out a plan it would be simple to slip away from this house.

One day, Zenji found the door to a locked room ajar. Careless, Ting.

He glanced down the hall. No one.

He slipped in. "Whoa," he whispered.

The room was packed with confiscated liquor, American

cigarettes, U.S. Army rations, and other valuable items. He picked up a bottle to read the label.

"Whatchoo doing!"

Zenji snapped around.

"Get out!" Ting shouted. "Now! I go whip!"

Zenji put the bottle back and gave Ting a knowing grin.

"I tell um, da co-nel! You in bad time. I tell um!"

"Go ahead," Zenji said. "Who cares? You're the one who forgot to lock the door."

But Zenji did care. Snooping could get him sent back to prison.

Colonel Fujimoto was enraged when Ting told him that Zenji had found his stash, but he didn't punish Zenji. After all, nothing was taken, and Ting had been careless, which the colonel made note of.

From that moment, Ting never missed a chance to berate Zenji.

"You stupid American! No can do nothing! I see dog more smart than you! I see donkey!"

Zenji stopped listening.

Ting had no power over him, as long as he didn't get caught snooping again.

There was still much he could learn here.

Time to be a better spy.

The months passed into 1944.

As far as Zenji could tell, the war was still going well for Japan. But Colonel Fujimoto was deeply concerned over the loss of an atoll called Truk, a key operational hub for Japan's Central and South Pacific defenses.

Though information was sketchy, Zenji was beginning to sense that the Americans were slowly getting the upper hand.

Colonel Fujimoto continued to have Zenji work at the office, which was more productive than searching the house. Still, Zenji had to be vigilant. One woman especially was always watching him.

But the colonel was a trusting man, and he seemed to like Zenji.

"You should join the Japanese army," he said one day. "Your country needs good workers like you."

"Thank you, sir, but I am still an American."

"Yes, but you are also one of us. You could be helpful. You have nowhere to go. Powerless. You might as well make the best of it."

"True. I am powerless."

"Think about it."

Zenji nodded. "I will."

And Zenji hoped he *could* be helpful. Just not to Japan.

But how could he get whatever he learned back to the army? The only Americans in Manila were POWs.

There had to be some way. He would find it.

By June 1944, he'd worked for Colonel Fujimoto for over a year. Ting remained suspicious, but he and Zenji had come to a mutual understanding that each was, in essence, a slave, and that there was not much they could do about it.

Zenji's time with Fujimoto had its good moments. The overworked colonel had come to trust him with sensitive chores. One was running papers from the colonel's office to other military offices, some actually outside the building. Zenji could have just disappeared.

But two things held him back: One, where would he go? Two, he still believed he could be of value to the U.S. by remaining where he was.

Strangest of all—Zenji had come to like Colonel Fujimoto. The colonel had even brought a man in to repair Zenji's glasses, and one evening, the colonel asked Zenji to join him for dinner at a nice restaurant. They talked of each other's home and family, and Zenji was surprised at how much they had in common, as Japanese men. For a couple of hours Zenji felt as if they were simply friends, or neighbors—just people.

It was good, and Zenji was glad that he'd waited.

Two months after that dinner, his big break walked in Colonel Fujimoto's door.

43

ISABEL NAVARRO

She was a small woman.

There was something about her, a focus that reminded Zenji of Aiko.

When none of the colonel's staff made any effort to help her, Zenji got up to guide her over to the colonel's office, where she waited for permission to enter.

Colonel Fujimoto ignored her. He was edgy that day. The U.S. had just taken Guam back, and that morning Zenji had overheard the office staff whispering about General MacArthur returning to the Philippines.

Return! Like he said he would.

Unconsciously, a grin had formed on Zenji's face. He caught himself and frowned.

Now the woman stood waiting at the office door.

Finally, the colonel snapped, *"Nani shini kitanda?"*

The woman hadn't understood.

Zenji stepped in. "He wants to know what you're here for."

"My husband . . ."

She spoke English. And she was nervous.

Zenji smiled. "Go on. I'll translate for you."

"I want to see my husband. He's in Muntinlupa Prison . . . they sent me here to get permission. Please, if you could only . . ."

She stopped and looked down.

"Let me see what I can do. Please, sit."

She sat, hands folded.

Zenji approached the colonel's desk. "Sir, this woman would like to visit her husband at the prison and needs your permission."

Colonel Fujimoto was in charge of the prison. It was one of his many duties, though he rarely visited the place himself. But he alone granted or denied all visitor passes. Zenji had seen every person who'd come in to request a visitation. There weren't a lot, and the colonel found them an annoyance.

"I'm too busy. Tell her no. Maybe in a week."

Zenji waited. He didn't want to give her bad news.

"Sir," he said. "I can help her. Let me take that weight off your shoulders. You have so much to do."

Colonel Fujimoto looked up.

"I'll move her along, sir."

"Fine. Take care of it."

"Thank you, sir."

Colonel Fujimoto got a permission slip out of a drawer and

handed it to Zenji. "Bring that back when you're done and I'll stamp it."

"Yes, sir."

Zenji returned to the woman and leaned close to speak low, in English. "Let's find a place where we can talk."

Her eyes slid past Zenji toward the colonel.

"Please," Zenji whispered, motioning to an empty desk away from the colonel's staff. They sat across from each other. People glanced up, but their eyes moved on.

"Now"—Zenji pulled out the permission form—"your name."

"Isabel Navarro."

"Husband?"

"Esteban Navarro."

"Why was he arrested?"

This question was not on the form. Zenji hoped that maybe he was one of the Filipino guerrillas allied with the U.S.— the guerrillas who made life miserable for the Japanese. If he was, Zenji might be able to establish a contact through him.

"A mistake. He is innocent."

"Innocent of what?"

She wouldn't say.

Zenji glanced back at the colonel, still working at his desk, head down. "Listen. I might be able to help you if I knew why he's in prison."

Mrs. Navarro said nothing.

"You can trust me," Zenji whispered.

She looked at her hands, clasped on the table.

Tell her, Zenji thought. What do you have to lose? "I'm an American prisoner. Forced to work here. You can trust me."

Zenji knew the question behind her narrowed eyes: American? You are Japanese. Do you think I'm stupid?

He touched her hand. "I give you my word, I'm telling the truth. Why else would I speak English so well? I'm from Hawaii."

She was silent.

"You have nothing to lose by telling me. The colonel already knows why he was arrested, not that he would ever tell me. But I might be able to help you."

Finally, she nodded and leaned close.

She had a lot to say. Zenji was astonished that she was so trusting. What she revealed was dangerous, and courageous. The colonel, it seemed, had no idea what went on in the prison.

Zenji stopped her in alarm. "Say nothing more. Not here. If they discover who your husband is they'll hang him. Never tell anyone this again."

Mrs. Navarro froze, as if she'd just killed her husband.

"No, no," Zenji said, seeing her fear. "Don't worry. I'm going to help you. I don't know how, but I'll figure it out."

What he'd learned was stunning.

Mrs. Navarro's husband was known as Nicodemo.

Zenji had heard the staff mention him. Nicodemo was a leader in the Filipino guerrilla movement who had smuggled valuable information to the Americans. The Japanese wanted him dead.

They had him and didn't even know it.

Zenji felt an instant kinship with this man.

His fingers began to tremble. This news was extremely heavy. She'd told him her husband had been an electrician before the war, and at the prison that skill had made him useful, so he had not been treated poorly.

Zenji's mind raced.

If he could get to the guerrillas, he could get to the Americans, and it might be possible for Nicodemo to smuggle information that could bring MacArthur back to Manila sooner rather than later.

Zenji stood. "Please wait."

He took the permission form to the colonel and placed it on his desk. Without reading it, Fujimoto reached into the drawer, pulled out his official *Han* stamp, and thumped it down.

"Thank you, sir."

The colonel tossed the stamp back into the drawer and closed it. Zenji took the form to Mrs. Navarro.

"I will escort you out," he whispered.

44
EIGHT TICKETS

Zenji and Mrs. Navarro stood under a clear blue sky. You'd never know there was a war going on. The streets were jammed with people and cars—just as before Japanese occupation.

They were lucky in Manila, Zenji thought, remembering the destruction on Corregidor.

He made sure no one was watching or close enough to hear. They found a bench and sat. "Mrs. Navarro, do you think your husband would talk to me?"

"Why?"

"We have a similar purpose," he said, low.

That was almost more than he wanted to say.

She shook her head. "He won't say a word to you, a Japanese."

"*American* Japanese. I told you, I'm a captive."

"How do I know that?"

"You just have to trust me, Mrs. Navarro."

She sat staring at the cars and bicycles going by. After a moment, she said, "I will see what I can do."

"I have an idea, a way to get you in to see your husband anytime you want."

She looked at him.

He handed her the stamped permission form. "Next time I'd like to go with you."

She glanced around.

Zenji couldn't blame her. He'd be suspicious, too. *Very* suspicious.

She walked away without looking back.

In the office, Zenji thought about the pass he'd given Mrs. Navarro. It was just a mimeographed form. He could roll those off all day long. It was the colonel's *Han* stamp that was important.

His plot began to grow.

A few days later he was alone in Colonel Fujimoto's office translating a captured American military communiqué. It made little sense. Must be code.

Even if he understood it he'd never give the colonel its real message. He'd provide a literal translation and let the colonel wrestle with its meaning.

The colonel was due back shortly.

Out in the open area only two clerks hunched over their desks, out of Zenji's view. By now the staff paid little attention to him.

Carrying the communiqué, Zenji faked a yawn and headed to the mimeograph machine, where a stack of prison permission slips sat on a shelf. He casually slipped some under the communiqué, and returned to his desk.

Neither clerk looked up.

He prayed the colonel was not on his way back.

Ten seconds. That's all he needed.

Do it!

He sprang over to the colonel's desk, opened the drawer with the *Han* stamp, and in a moment of jittery exhilaration, stamped eight permission forms, stuffed them down his shirt, replaced the stamp, and returned to his desk.

His knees shook. Sweat rolled down his side.

Focus.

He gasped, startled when he heard the colonel's voice. "Give it to me."

Zenji looked up.

"The communiqué. You've translated it?"

"Yes, sir." He handed it over, sweat soaking the prison passes inside his shirt.

Mrs. Navarro returned a few weeks later. Zenji jumped up to greet her before anyone else could, not that they would even notice her.

"Good afternoon, Mrs. Navarro. How can we help you today?"

She smiled. "I would like permission to visit my husband again."

"Certainly," Zenji said. "Colonel Fujimoto is a generous man. Let's fill out another permission form."

Mrs. Navarro sat at Zenji's desk while he filled out the

form. He took it to the colonel, who stamped it and waved Zenji away.

At his desk, Zenji opened his drawer and placed the stamped form on top of the eight *Han*-stamped ones he'd hidden there. He fought to keep his fingers from shaking as he pushed the forms toward Mrs. Navarro, keeping one for himself just in case he needed it.

Her breath caught.

Zenji smiled.

She quickly folded them and stood.

As before, Zenji escorted her from the office.

"May I join you in your visit?" he said low, looking straight ahead.

"Yes."

Zenji stopped and turned to her. "Wait here, Mrs. Navarro. I need to ask permission to escort you."

"But—"

"He will allow it. He's relieved that I've taken on the business of dealing with the prison."

Zenji inquired and got another dismissive wave from Colonel Fujimoto.

He left before the colonel had time to think about the access he'd just given to an American prisoner.

He's too good for war, Zenji thought.

Too trusting.

Not that the Bamboo Rat was complaining.

45

ESTEBAN NAVARRO

Esteban Navarro would not look at Zenji.

His wife motioned for them to move away from the guards, who were lounging on folding chairs near the barred entrance. Seven other men sat with visitors at picnic tables scattered around the caged visiting area.

Lazy guards.

Good.

They'd been half-asleep at the prison entry shack, too. Heat and humidity did that to you.

If Colonel Fujimoto knew how lazy his guards were, he'd double their number, at least.

They sat at a table.

Finally, Esteban gave Zenji a look that could peel paint off a house. "I regret allowing this meeting," he whispered.

"He just wants to talk to you, Esteban."

"Of course he does. They're always trying to get me to confess to things I have not done. I'm innocent!"

Zenji knew that bit was for him.

"Esteban, I *told* you. He's American."

"She's right," Zenji said, low. "From Honolulu. And I know that you are Nicodemo."

Navarro's face turned bright red. Veins thickened in his neck and the knuckles in his fists turned white.

Mrs. Navarro didn't flinch.

Zenji whispered, "If I was one of *them* would you still be here? I would have taken the glory of turning you in and you'd be in a box under six feet of dirt. We fight on the same side, Mr. Navarro."

Navarro glanced toward the lazy guards, then at his wife.

She nodded, eyes unwavering.

Navarro crossed his arms and sat back. "If you lie, you will die."

"I understand."

Zenji checked the guards. Probably think I'm a Japanese official.

"My wife says you work for Fujimoto," Navarro said. "Why? If you are who you say you are."

"I'm a prisoner. They use me to interpret. But they have gotten lazy, and I have freedoms that I shouldn't have. I've convinced them that I'm a civilian with little interest in the war. They are mildly suspicious, but not vigilant."

"He helped me, Esteban," Mrs. Navarro said. "Look." She quickly showed him the eight folded permission slips. "He stole Fujimoto's stamp."

240

She hid the slips again.

"What do you have to lose by trusting me?" Zenji pleaded. "You're already in prison. If I was going to turn you in, I would have done it already. What more can they do?"

"Execute me."

"And me, if this plan is discovered."

"What plan?"

Yes, what plan? At first Zenji had only wanted to get information out by way of the guerrillas. But after seeing the careless security, and how the guards treated him as though he was a person of authority, another plan was brewing.

Zenji leaned close. "You still have men on the outside?"

"Maybe."

"You want to get out?"

Navarro grunted.

"I think I can help."

Navarro slid his gaze over Zenji's shoulder at the guards. "Go on."

Zenji rubbed his chin. A plan was growing, so audacious it made his stomach flutter. "Can you get me five men? On the outside . . . Filipinos who look Japanese?"

"Possibly."

"You're an electrician?"

"I keep the lights on."

"Is it possible for you to shut this place down at night? Cut the power?"

"Poof," Esteban said.

The guards stood. Visiting time was up.

Zenji whispered, "Can your guys on the outside get some Japanese uniforms? Without blood on them?"

For the first time, Esteban Navarro smiled.

Zenji quickly told him his plan.

It took more than a month to get everything in place.

With Mrs. Navarro as his guide, Zenji met quietly with five nervous men in a secluded area of a nearby park. Without her, Zenji never would have gotten near these men.

Each man had a part in Zenji's plan. He smiled, thinking how easily they could pass for Japanese soldiers.

"We have only one shot," Zenji said. "And if we fail it won't go well for any of us."

"We will die to get Nicodemo out," one man said.

Esteban's wife frowned. "No one dies."

Zenji nodded. "I'm counting on that, Mrs. Navarro."

The most important piece in Zenji's plan was also the most dangerous to acquire: a red sash, signifying Officer of the Day status.

He knew where he could find one: in a supply room on the floor above Fujimoto's office. He prayed that there would be a few of them so that one would not be missed.

Without the sash the plan wouldn't work.

Zenji had been sent to the supply room long ago to obtain unmarked military clothing for himself, which he wore whenever making deliveries outside the building.

But the stern clerk who manned the supply room was fussy about every item.

Zenji steeled himself for what he was about to do. If he failed it could be the end of his freedom.

He left the office as if to head to the restroom, and ran up the stairs.

The supply-room clerk sat at his gray metal desk, his pencil perfectly aligned with the edge, six inches in. "Yes?"

"I need a new pair of pants," Zenji said. "I spilled ink on my only pair. Can't get the stain out."

"Bring them to me."

"I can't. I gave them to a beggar on the street."

For a moment the clerk was speechless. "Those pants did not belong to you."

Zenji nodded. "I will pay for them."

"You certainly will." The clerk stood. "Size?"

"Twenty-eight-inch waist, thirty-one-inch length."

They passed through a maze of metal shelving to get to the uniforms. Zenji saw the sashes on a shelf. Grab one now!

But the clerk kept glancing back at him.

Zenji passed by the sashes.

The clerk pulled a pair of pants from a stack. Zenji held them to his waist and nodded. "Perfect."

The clerk headed back to the front.

The red sashes leaped out at Zenji as he approached them again. Sweat broke out over his scalp.

The clerk glanced back. "Come on, come on."

The second the clerk turned, Zenji grabbed a sash and stuffed it inside his shirt. His hands were shaking so bad he had to put them in his pockets and carry the pants under his arm.

The clerk turned back and held out his hand.

Zenji nearly fainted.

"Pay me. For the pants you gave away."

Zenji fumbled some cash out. "That enough?"

The clerk gathered it up and put it in his drawer without counting it.

Zenji was certain that he'd overpaid. He hoped he had. The clerk would probably pocket the extra cash, and a guilty clerk would keep his mouth shut.

"Go," the clerk said.

Back on his floor, Zenji hid in the bathroom until he could stop shaking.

On the evening his plan was to go down, Zenji lay sweating on his mattress in the dark. Sleep was impossible, not that he'd even considered it.

Just past midnight he got up and peeked down the hall. Colonel Fujimoto slept on the floor above, and never showed his face before six in the morning.

But what about Ting?

Zenji dressed quickly in civilian clothes.

From under his mattress, he pulled out the neatly folded Japanese uniform he'd stolen from the colonel's collection. Zenji would have it back in the closet before anyone noticed it was gone.

He'd also stolen an officer's insignia and a pin to make the uniform look official. With the red sash, no one would question him.

He bundled everything under his arm and peeked down the hall.

Clear.

Holding his breath, Zenji crept out into the night.

The five guerrillas were waiting in the bushes in regular Japanese army uniforms. Zenji inspected them for blood and knife holes.

Clean.

He quickly changed into his uniform and hid his clothes in the bushes. "The others in place?"

The men nodded.

"Let's go."

They headed out.

Henry would think he'd lost his mind. Maybe he had.

Thinking of Henry gave him courage.

"I'll do the talking," he said, putting on the red sash.

They marched toward the prison.

As they approached, two armed guards stepped out to block them. But when they saw Zenji they bowed and backed off.

Zenji was astounded.

The guerrillas quickly overcame, bound, and gagged the guards, and forced them to their knees.

One guerrilla pulled a knife.

"No!" Zenji snapped. "It will enrage the Japanese to find dead guards. Hide them. Get the others. Go!"

As two men dragged the guards into the entry shack, a wave of thirty ghostly guerrillas rose up out of the bushes nearby and silently scurried toward the gate.

They followed Zenji to the prison armory, which they quickly secured. He left ten men to empty it. The weapons would go to the guerrillas.

Zenji checked his watch.

Thirty seconds had passed.

"Come on, come on," he whispered.

Foomp!

Every light in the prison went out.

"Let's go!"

They were quick.

First, they secured every guard in the prison, then ran from cell to cell, releasing Navarro and his guerrillas. The hardened criminals shouted at them, but they were left behind.

In less than twenty minutes, five hundred men scattered into the night.

Esteban Navarro clamped a hand on Zenji's shoulder. "My friend, I won't forget this. Good luck."

"How can I contact you?"

"My wife."

Navarro ran into the dark.

Zenji found his hidden clothes, changed, and ran back to the mansion, his footfalls soft.

He hid the sash and the colonel's uniform in the garage. He'd return the uniform, except for the sash, which he would destroy the first chance he got.

He removed his shoes and eased open the kitchen door.

The house was silent.

He crept toward his room, stopping to peer in on the Taiwanese in their bunk room.

Ting was missing.

46

OUTRAGE

Zenji slipped into his closet bedroom, then staggered back.

Ting crouched near his mattress with a machete. "Where you went, stupid American?"

Slowly, Zenji set his shoes down. "None of your business."

"You tell. Where you went?"

"To the bathroom."

Ting snorted. "T'ree-hour piss?"

Zenji shrugged and started unbuttoning his shirt.

"You no tell me, I tell Fujimoto. Or . . . maybe I jus' kill you."

"I went for a walk. Couldn't sleep."

"I see you go. You take something. Where it went, what you took?"

Zenji flicked the accusation off with a wave of his hand. "Listen," he said with a sigh. "I . . . I just met someone."

"Who?"

"I have . . . a girlfriend . . . if you must know."

Ting seemed surprised. He grinned and kissed his fingers. "Filipina?"

"Beat it," Zenji said. "I'm tired."

Ting stayed where he was for another minute, then stood. "I go, but still, I tell."

The next day, Colonel Fujimoto headed off in his limousine. Nothing seemed out of the ordinary.

But where was Ting?

Zenji checked the bunk room.

Nothing but Ting's unmade bed and dirty laundry.

Zenji yawned, exhausted from worry and his brazen deed. How could he have even thought of such an insane thing, much less done it? *Five hundred* guerrillas! When Fujimoto found out he would explode!

Get to the office. Quick!

He hurried into his room and slammed into Ting. "What are you doing in here?"

Ting grinned, and pulled a folded piece of paper from his back pocket. He opened it.

Zenji's extra *Han*-stamped prison permission form!

Zenji snatched it.

"Give um!" Ting tried to get the form back. Zenji ripped it to shreds and stuffed the pieces into his pocket.

Ting ran to get his machete.

Zenji raced out the door to the bus stop.

* * *

When Zenji arrived at the office he took a moment to compose himself before walking in.

Just another morning.

No one looked up, as usual.

Colonel Fujimoto was at his desk. Clearly, he had not yet heard.

Zenji felt pings of terror in his gut.

He made tea as always, carried it in to the colonel, set it on his desk.

Fujimoto did not look up.

Zenji headed to his desk and picked through a new stack of documents to be translated. He forced himself to keep his head down, hard at work.

An officer burst in, ran through to Colonel Fujimoto's office.

Everyone looked up.

"Colonel!" the man shouted.

Colonel Fujimoto stood.

The staff, Zenji included, looked from one to another and got up to crowd around the door to the colonel's office. Zenji acted mystified, alarmed.

As the story tumbled out, the colonel's face reddened. He slammed his fist on the desk. "How did this *happen*?"

The man, probably the prison director, cowered. "No one knows."

"You left the armory *unguarded*? Filipinos? Out! Out!"

The man bowed and backed away.

"Out!" the colonel shouted again. "Out! Out!"

The staff scattered when Colonel Fujimoto raged into the open area. Zenji held his breath, afraid even to blink.

"Call my car!" the colonel snapped. "Now!"

Zenji grabbed the phone and dialed.

Colonel Fujimoto paced, shouting at his staff, spitting out details of the prison break.

Zenji pretended to be as shocked as everyone else.

His staff listened, frozen, terrified.

When the colonel stormed out, Zenji sagged against a wall, dizzy.

THE AUDACITY OF COURAGE

The only facts the colonel ever uncovered were that a prisoner named Navarro had shut the prison's electrical system down, that six men disguised as Japanese soldiers had overtaken the gate guards, that close to fifty men had slipped in to release the guerrillas, and the most unbearable disgrace: the looting of his armory.

Colonel Fujimoto demanded that the perpetrators be captured and executed.

Zenji had never been so scared in his life.

Because there was one glaring clue that the colonel was overlooking: the leader of the disguised Japanese soldiers was Japanese and had worn a red sash. If the colonel had thought it through he would have wondered where that man might have laid hands on one.

But so far it didn't look like the colonel had thought of such things. Now it was all about cleaning up the mess.

Ting worried Zenji even more than the colonel. If he ever told Fujimoto what he knew about that night, Zenji would have to run.

But Ting kept quiet.

Why?

One evening, Zenji found himself in the kitchen with Ting and Cheng, the cook. Ting was slicing onions for the colonel's dinner.

Zenji edged up. "Ting," he said, low.

As usual, Ting refused to look directly at Zenji.

Zenji glanced at Cheng. He needed privacy.

But Cheng spoke no English.

Zenji went on. He had to know.

"I, uh . . . I want to thank you . . . for not telling, you know, about that night."

Ting looked up. He glared, but his face softened. He shook his head and went back to slicing.

Zenji waited, not knowing how to say what he needed to say. The last thing he wanted to do was give Ting more information than he had to. But he sensed that Ting knew that he had something to do with the escape, and he had to know if Ting would keep quiet. If Ting's silence was in question, Zenji would disappear.

Was that even possible?

Manila was full of alleys and warrens and places to hide. But he would need help, and no Filipino civilians were going to help a Japanese. And the guerillas were in the hills.

Ting flicked his chin at Zenji. "I no tell because you like me, like Cheng, like driver."

Cheng looked up, hearing his name.

Zenji cocked his head. "What you mean?"

"Slave," Ting said.

Relief made Zenji near giddy. He smiled. "Right."

Ting nodded.

From that moment on Zenji and Colonel Fujimoto's servants became comrades. Not friends, but it was enough.

A few weeks later, Mrs. Navarro showed up at the office. What audacity! What courage! Was she crazy?

Zenji had thought he'd never see her again.

Colonel Fujimoto spotted her, put his hands on his desk, and slowly stood. He kept his eyes on her as he strutted into the open area.

"You," the colonel said. "Your husband is the one who turned off the power and helped dangerous men escape. Where is he?"

He still doesn't know he'd had a major resistance leader in the palm of his hand.

The colonel was nearly removed from his position over the loss of five hundred prisoners of war. If it had been discovered that he'd also lost Nicodemo, he would have been dishonorably dismissed and shamed to his grave.

Zenji translated the colonel's question.

"I am here to learn that myself," Mrs. Navarro said in English. "I am worried about him. He's just a poor electrician, imprisoned by mistake. You must find him."

Brilliant, Zenji thought as he translated for the colonel. This makes her seem completely innocent. One who helped orchestrate an escape would *never* return.

The colonel's eyes narrowed as he listened. Zenji guessed

that he'd love to throw Mrs. Navarro in prison to satisfy his loss of face.

But he was much too honorable for that.

He turned to Zenji. "Escort this woman from this building and tell her never to return. If she does I will have her arrested."

Zenji bowed and took Mrs. Navarro by her elbow. "Come."

"Did you see the look on his face?" she whispered as they headed down the hall.

Zenji looked straight ahead.

"Esteban says that he will be forever grateful for your courage. And he wants to know if you have information."

Zenji smiled. "I will."

After that, Zenji was able to pass what he knew on to the guerrillas through Mrs. Navarro, hoping it would end up in American hands. He never wrote anything down, but memorized communiqués about troop movements around Manila, shipping information, reports on a Japanese force on the southern tip of Mindanao.

The guerrillas had to keep moving. The Japanese Signal Corps was able to monitor their radio transmissions and trace their locations.

Since all information having to do with the escaped men went through Colonel Fujimoto's office, Zenji was able to keep Navarro and his men aware of every move the Japanese made in their efforts to locate and trap them.

But the Japanese would never be successful. There were over two hundred thousand guerrillas throughout the Philippines. Nicodemo's unit was only one small part of a vast organization.

Colonel Fujimoto never accused Zenji of anything, but Zenji believed a shadow of suspicion sat in the back of the colonel's mind. He'd become colder, formal, but that could have been due to his disgrace.

Zenji knew that soon none of it would matter, anyway.

The Americans were coming back.

He could hear it in office whispers, smell it in the air, feel it in his bones.

48

LEAVING THE WEASEL

By late September 1944, American air raids into Japanese-held territory had grown bolder. Colonel Fujimoto and the Fourteenth Army headquarters were forced to move to more bomb-secure Fort McKinley, south of the city.

The colonel and his staff could not believe that Japan was unable to stop the Americans. And worse, Japan had lost its bases in the Mariana Islands. From there, American bombers could reach Japan!

How was this possible? Japan was a far superior force.

Colonel Fujimoto hardly paid attention to Zenji.

Zenji had to be alert to any opportunity to escape.

"Ting," he whispered one evening, "you know it's coming to an end soon?"

"Not for us." Ting lifted his chin toward the cook.

"The Americans are coming," Zenji said. "Fujimoto will have to leave Manila. You can escape."

Ting stared at the floor. "Nowhere to go."

"You can find help among the people of—"

"They no like."

Probably true. Anyone who worked for the Japanese would be scorned.

"Still," Zenji said. "Be prepared."

Ting nodded. "You watch, too, American."

"Yeah. Dangerous. I look like the enemy, ah?"

Ting ran a finger across his throat.

"Seen that before," Zenji said.

But Ting was right. If he were to escape and remain in Manila, the invading Americans could mistake him for the enemy and shoot him on the spot. If he were to stay with Colonel Fujimoto, he could be executed as his usefulness to Japan diminished.

But to be *free*.

The word took him by surprise.

For a moment he even allowed himself to think of returning home. A swelling rose in his throat, almost bringing him to tears. He hadn't allowed himself to feel how much he missed his family—Ma, Akio, Henry.

He had not tortured himself with this thought.

No, he told himself. This is not the time to get your hopes up. You are surrounded by desperate men who would kill you in a second—Japanese, Filipino, and even your own guys.

* * *

"Watanabe!" Colonel Fujimoto called one day from his office. "Get this place packed up. We're leaving Manila. Now! Now!"

"Yes, sir! Where do I start?"

"I don't care. Just do it."

He's coming unglued, Zenji thought, and he knew why. General Yamashita, the mastermind behind the fall of Singapore, had replaced the ineffective General Kuroda, and had taken command in the Pacific. Not everyone supported Yamashita's decision to evacuate Manila. Many wanted to stay and fight to the death.

Yamashita's plan was to move his command to Baguio, a summer city one hundred thirty miles north of Manila, five thousand feet above sea level in the mountains of Luzon.

"Ting, you gotta run," Zenji pleaded, back at the mansion. "Fujimoto no need you now. Worse if you stay."

Ting shook his head. "We run, Filipino kill."

Maybe Ma was right about those machetes.

Zenji was still useful to the colonel, so was not dismissed to the same fate as the Taiwanese, who were assigned to the Fourteenth Army Labor Battalion to spend their days with picks, shovels, and machetes, clearing the way for the retreat to Baguio.

I warned you, Zenji thought as the three men were herded toward a troop transport.

Ting turned to Zenji. "Good luck, American slave."

"And you, weasel."

"What is weasel?"

"A smart hunter."

Ting nodded once.

They left with what little they owned, which was almost nothing. As the truck lumbered away, Zenji called, "You no make um back home safe, I whip!"

Ting grinned.

Zenji knew he was being watched.

He did his best to blend in, especially since the officers who worked with Colonel Fujimoto looked upon him with increasing hatred. They'd have had the American traitor shot long ago.

Escape. Soon.

But not in Manila.

Now Zenji climbed into the back of a commandeered covered fruit truck that was Colonel Fujimoto's moving van. It was packed with files and belongings. Zenji could barely squeeze in.

The driver tossed him a clean medical mask. "You may need it."

"Thanks."

He secured it over his mouth and nose. The drive would be dusty. He'd be covered in grime by the time they got to Baguio.

The Japanese units that remained behind would be brutal. Leaving with Fujimoto was the best choice.

It's crazy, Zenji thought as they drove away. Bamboo Rat still lives among the enemy. What about Spider?

Is he still in Australia?

And had Benny Suzuki found his way to his family?

One day at a time.

For now—be indispensable. Then, safely in Baguio—escape. Hide in the jungle until the Japanese are defeated, emerge, and reunite with his countrymen.

This was all he thought about on the long, grinding journey.

BAGUIO

Zenji was surprised to find Baguio completely untouched by war, even now, in late 1944. It was a city of low buildings, beautiful trees, and wide, clean streets, with little traffic. And it was cool, a relief from Manila.

Peaceful like Honolulu. Until General Yamashita's convoy rolled into town. The general set up headquarters in the Baguio hospital. Colonel Fujimoto, Zenji, and staff occupied a nearby church.

"Can you cook?" Colonel Fujimoto asked Zenji.

"Yes, sir."

He'd never cooked anything but meat and fish on a small hibachi, and only when Ma had told him to.

"Good. You are now a cook. In fact, you are now my entire house staff." The colonel eked out a rare smile.

"Yes, sir!" Zenji gave him a salute.

The colonel still stood tall. He was an enemy, but Zenji knew he was a decent man. He cared about people. Probably why he had a desk job.

Cooking turned out to be a good assignment. The colonel received foods that most did not, like rice and even sweets. Provisions were very low, with little hope of a supply line to replenish what was consumed. Japanese troops had to forage in the jungle.

Good, Zenji thought. If they can forage, so can I.

He was running out of time.

Jungle survival. He started hiding small amounts of uncooked rice and other things that would not spoil. But food became scarce.

"This is all?" the colonel snapped one evening.

Zenji had served him a child's portion of rice.

"Rations are few, Colonel."

"This rice is not thoroughly cooked. You are incompetent!" Colonel Fujimoto pushed his plate aside.

"Yes, sir. Sorry, sir." Zenji bowed.

The colonel glared.

"You are not paying attention to your duties. You must do better!"

He slapped the table and stood.

Zenji bowed. "I will work harder, Colonel. I promise."

The colonel stormed away.

Please him! Escape depends on the freedom he gives you. *Do better.*

Weeks passed into 1945. April.

Zenji's cooking improved, but Colonel Fujimoto flew into

fits over the smallest disruptions. The war had moved into the islands of Okinawa, where Zenji's parents were from. And Manila was now a raging war zone. The Americans were winning, and would soon head toward Baguio and other parts of Luzon. Yamashita was making plans to retreat even deeper into the mountains.

Zenji knew they would all be starving, and wouldn't waste food on him.

Time to run.

Days later, as the Japanese prepared to evacuate Baguio, Zenji found himself alone in the church. The colonel had ordered him to destroy all remaining files and pack everything else.

Zenji stole a courier's pouch and filled it with what he'd hidden away. Grains of rice, a handful of rations.

What else, what else?

A bowl. A spoon.

A kitchen knife.

A small first-aid kit.

A pistol!

He found it in the colonel's room. He had no idea what kind it was, and he could find no ammunition. He'd have to live with whatever ammo was already loaded.

He jammed the pistol into the pouch and placed it in a box, which he hid in the pile of discarded boxes from the destroyed files. No one would look there.

Two nights later, a grim colonel gathered his staff in the church. "Manila has fallen. The Americans are coming here. We leave in three days to fight them in the hills. Anything you can't carry, destroy."

Manila has fallen!

"You!" Colonel Fujimoto snapped at Zenji. "Build a fire. Burn everything."

Zenji's eyes slid toward the pile of empty boxes.

"Not those. Only what the enemy might use. Now!"

"Yes, sir!" Zenji said. Thank God, the colonel still thought of him as one of his own.

He got a fire going.

It stayed alive for two full days as they burned everything that should not fall into the hands of the enemy.

Zenji's stash remained hidden in the pile of rubbish.

How would he retrieve it when the time came?

As he tended the fire, fear nearly overcame him.

He was so *close*.

He began to sweat.

The colonel noticed. "What's wrong with you?"

Zenji froze.

The colonel came closer.

"I . . . sir . . . I'm . . . I'm sick."

"Sick?"

The colonel stepped back.

"Yes, sir. It started last night. Don't get close. I wouldn't want you to catch it. . . . It will pass soon."

Another plan brewed.

50

INTO THE FOG

The next morning Zenji was awakened by a kick from one of the staff. "Up!"

He nodded and rose to his elbows.

The colonel appeared. "We leave in an hour."

Zenji looked up with heavy eyes. "My sickness . . . worse, sir."

The colonel squatted and placed his hand on Zenji's forehead. He frowned. "Can you walk?"

Zenji faked an effort to sit, but fell back. "I'm sorry, sir. Too weak . . . leave me. I will recover . . . and find you."

"Colonel!" someone called. "They're moving."

"Kobayashi!" the colonel shouted.

Kobayashi, a spineless clerk who had never been friendly to Zenji, hurried over. "Sir?"

265

"Watanabe has a fever. Stay with him until he is better. Give him no more than one day to recover, then both of you catch up with us."

"Stay *here,* sir?"

"One day! No more," the colonel snapped.

"Yes, sir."

"Go find a weapon. You know how to shoot?"

"No, sir. I'm an office worker."

"It's easy. Pull the trigger."

Colonel Fujimoto turned back to Zenji, who lay looking helplessly ill on his cot. "One day. Is that clear? No choice. You will rejoin us. Kobayashi will see to it. If the Filipinos don't shoot you, he will."

Zenji knew he would, too, but he was surprised to hear such harsh words from the colonel. Desperation.

He gave the colonel a weak but grateful look. "Oh, yes, sir. We will find you."

The colonel hurried out.

With luck, Zenji thought, we will never meet again.

By the end of the day every Japanese soldier in Baguio was gone. Only Kobayashi remained.

And a whole city of unfriendly citizens.

The next morning Kobayashi was near frantic. He hadn't slept at all. "I can't wait. You're not worth it!" He touched the pistol tucked under his belt.

Zenji kept his mouth shut. Kobayashi could easily shoot him and tell Fujimoto that Zenji had tried to escape.

"Get up! We're going."

Zenji started to get up, thinking: I could take that gun away.

Don't chance it.

"Too sick," he said.

Kobayashi pulled the pistol and aimed it at Zenji's face. "We're leaving! Now!"

Zenji gambled on Kobayashi's weakness. "Sick . . . shoot me."

Kobayashi's hand shook, and dropped.

He simply ran.

Zenji gave him ten minutes.

He leaped off the cot and pulled his pouch from the pile of boxes, then searched for anything else he could use.

Nights would be cold. He grabbed the thin blanket off his cot, slung it over his shoulder, and secured it under the pouch strap.

Outside, a fog had set in. The people of Baguio had begun to emerge. They'd kept out of sight while their town had been occupied.

Zenji was a free man for the first time in over two years.

He jogged through the foggy streets along the edge of the trees, looking for a trail into the vast jungle where he could hide.

He could find only thin paths made by animals.

He picked one and followed it into the pine trees.

The pines dipped into ravines and the landscape soon turned into a much thicker jungle. The fog burned off and sunlight streamed down through the canopy, splattering flecks of light over the knee-high understory. Vines fell like ropes, twisting around trees, threatening to choke them.

The jungle murmured with the sounds of birds, insects,

toads, bats, and what all else, he had no clue. Were there poisonous spiders and snakes on this island?

Be alert. Be sharp.

In a way, Zenji found the jungle beautiful, as he pushed deeper and deeper in.

After an hour he stopped and looked around. Which way was he heading? His sense of direction was off. He needed a compass and hadn't thought to find one before leaving.

Not smart.

He pushed ahead, concerned, but not discouraged. He slowed as the jungle became wilder, more impenetrable. Now he knew why Filipinos carried machetes.

The sun was barely visible. He hoped its arc would give him directional clues. But the trees were so thick.

For all he knew he was heading right back to Baguio.

By the time night fell he was hopelessly lost.

He stumbled into a small clearing and sat, completely exhausted. Living with the colonel had made him soft.

He took off his glasses and cleaned them on a corner of the blanket. Daylight was soon gone.

The darkness was deeper than any he'd ever known. He could not see a single star, nor was there the slightest glow, anywhere.

Noises.

He needed a fire.

He had a few matches, but he'd forgotten to think about gathering something to burn while there was still enough light to see. On hands and knees he felt the ground around him.

Nothing.

He reached into his pouch, searching for something to eat. A few stale crackers.

He ate, tongue dry. Parched.

The water in the canteen was all he'd thought to carry. Bad planning. He should have spent more time considering jungle survival. He'd just figured he would drink from a stream.

There was no stream.

The water tasted like silk, cool and clean. But he couldn't have much, not until he had a source to replace what he drank. He screwed the cap on extra tight, savoring what little water he'd taken in.

The temperature dropped, and he wrapped the blanket around his shoulders. That first night in the jungle, Zenji slept less than an hour. The rest of it was filled with bugs crawling over him, terrifying unidentifiable noises, and impenetrable darkness.

Was it possible to get lost and never find your way out?

When the jungle began to reappear early the next morning, Zenji's courage returned as well. Why, he wondered, did darkness bring such debilitating fear, and hope return with daylight?

Light and dark were more powerful than he'd ever imagined.

First thing, he searched for firewood, gathering twigs and small broken branches, none dry enough to burn. He'd have to find sunny spots where the heat would evaporate the moisture before dark.

He stuffed the sticks into his pouch and slung his blanket over his shoulder. Which way to go?

No trails.

He sucked in a deep breath and shoved ahead. Don't fight it. Losing battle, now and forever. Simply move in directions offered by the landscape.

On the second night he managed a small fire. He boiled rice, using the least amount of canteen water possible.

He ate and collapsed into sleep, and the next morning got up and forged on, to where, he had no idea.

On the third night as he made his small fire, he sensed something nearby.

He sat without moving.

Something.

Human. He couldn't explain why.

He stood and squinted into the darkness. "Who's there?"

Dancing reflections from the fire, nothing more.

It was too quiet. The usual night noises had been replaced by a stillness that made his skin crawl.

Slowly, Zenji eased down and snuffed out the fire.

He moved away from the embers, sat, and listened, blanket tight around him.

Hours passed.

Finally, he slept.

At dawn he awoke with a spear point resting on his heart.

RED TEETH

They were small men with red teeth, wearing loincloths and a thin cloak over one shoulder.

How many? Ten? Twenty? Zenji was too scared to count.

A man with Zenji's pistol stood behind the one with the spear, holding the gun loosely.

Zenji rose to his elbows, his eyes locked onto the man's whose spear touched his skin.

Were these the mountain people he'd read about? Who lived deep in the jungle and didn't like to be seen? Farmers, who hunted? Not headhunters. Please, no.

The man with the spear stepped back. More men silently appeared. They had hair that hung to their ears, cut off evenly all the way around.

Zenji got to his knees, and slowly stood.

The man with the spear reached out and touched Zenji's chest, as if to see if he was real.

He turned to his men and spoke.

The man turned back to Zenji. *"Toy edapo-an mo?"*

Zenji smiled. Be friendly.

"Nganto y ngagan mo?" the man said.

Zenji shook his head. What?

The man tapped his own chest. "Abir." He nodded to Zenji.

"Abir," Zenji repeated, and the man smiled, red teeth gleaming. He tapped his chest again.

Zenji grinned, and tapped his own chest. "Zenji."

The men repeated it, laughing at how hard it was to say the letter Z.

"Seh'si! Seh'si!" they chanted, making sweeping motions, as if in their language *Zenji* meant "broom."

Zenji played along, sweeping the ground.

The men giggled.

If they were headhunters, they were happy ones.

Abir cautiously touched Zenji's glasses.

"Glasses," Zenji said, taking them off and letting Abir hold them.

Abir put them on. He squinted and took them off, shaking his head, handing them back.

Zenji laughed.

Abir motioned for Zenji to follow them.

Zenji hesitated.

Abir motioned again, smiling.

I'm so lost I'd probably die, anyway, Zenji thought. I'm hungry. Need water. My canteen is empty.

He'd have to trust that they wouldn't shrink his head or boil him in a tub.

He followed the red-toothed men deeper into the jungle on a trail so slight that he would never have picked it up. But there it was. How was it that he'd never spotted anything like a path? They were probably all over the place, yet known only to these men.

Soon they came to a village of wood-sided huts with heavily grassed roofs. Old men, children, and women stopped what they were doing and froze.

He smiled at them.

Abir said something to Zenji, raising his fingers to his mouth.

Ah, yes. Zenji nodded. He *was* hungry.

Using his hands, Zenji asked for a drink.

Abir beamed and ran off to return with a wooden bowl of clear water.

Zenji drank deeply as the villagers watched.

He felt like some lost soul from the streets of Manila. He was filthy. Probably smelled like a garbage can.

Zenji handed the empty bowl back, and Abir motioned for Zenji to follow him to a hut. He nodded toward the entry.

"Go in?" Zenji pointed to the opening.

Abir nodded.

Zenji crawled through the small entrance.

Inside, the hard-packed dirt floor was swept clean. There was a mat and another bowl of water.

He crawled back out.

Abir mimicked sleeping, and made snoring sounds, which got a big laugh out of everyone.

Zenji figured he was saying, *Take a nap.* "Thank you." He crawled back in. Someone sat by the entry, either to guard him or to attend to his needs.

He fell asleep before he could figure it out.

It was evening when he awoke.

Outside, Abir had been sitting on a rock staring at the hut. *"Mayatya davi."*

"Yeah," Zenji said, standing. "Sounds good." He rubbed his face. "How long did I sleep?"

Abir grinned. He was probably the happiest guy Zenji had ever met.

The sun had set, but the sky still held some light.

Abir led Zenji to what looked like a feast.

A fire, bowls of food.

Abir had Zenji sit next to him. The men who'd found him in the jungle clumped around them, munching on red nuts. *That's* what colored their teeth.

A man brought a large bowl to Abir, who seemed to be the leader, or chief, though he looked only thirty or so.

Abir took the bowl and with his fingers scooped up a small portion of food. He ate and those around him nodded in apparent satisfaction.

He handed the bowl to Zenji.

Zenji took the bowl and looked into it. Rice, soaked in . . . blood?

He glanced at Abir, who grinned and motioned for Zenji to partake. For a second Zenji thought he'd pass the bowl on. But he couldn't dishonor or embarrass Abir.

He scooped up a portion the same size as Abir had taken. It was warm. Faking delight, Zenji sucked the rice off his fingers, tasting the metallic tang of blood. He struggled to keep from gagging, swallowing quickly, thinking of the harbor at Honolulu, the stars in the sky at night, Aiko, Freddy, Benny, dancing with Mina, anything to take his mind off his buzzing taste buds.

He smiled and passed the bowl to the man next to him.

And so it went, the bowl passing from man to man until it was empty.

The tang of blood remained on his tongue.

When the feast began, he ate and ate.

The next round of rice had no blood, and was the best rice he'd ever had in his life. He had no idea what the meat was. He leaned close to the man next to him and pointed at it.

"What is this?"

The man grinned, as if to say the meat was indeed good, served only on special occasions.

Zenji said, "But what *is* it? Goat?" He mimicked small horns and a goatee with his fingers.

The man laughed and pointed at a dog with his chin.

Dog?

They were eating *dog*!

Hold it, he told himself.

This is *not* Nami!

He closed his eyes and sat with that thought for a moment. He was starving. The food was keeping him alive, and for that he was grateful.

After the feast, Zenji thanked Abir over and over.

This seemed to please Abir.

Sleeping in the hut with no worry of snakes was as good as sleeping in his bed at home.

* * *

The next day he studied the movement of the sun, trying to discern direction. Where was he? Which way should he go? If these people would let him go.

He tried to ask Abir where Baguio was, but Abir waved generally in all directions, as if to say *everywhere*.

Not working.

Zenji sighed and nodded thanks anyway.

He stayed with Abir's people for a month, as far as he could tell. Maybe more.

During that time he watched what the mountain people ate and where they got their food and water. He had to learn survival skills before he left. If it took him weeks to find his way out, and it probably would, at least he would stand a better chance if he knew a few things.

He tried to get his pistol back, pointing his finger like a gun. But as before, Abir just smiled and waved in every direction.

Occasionally, Zenji heard gunfire in the distant hills. American forces must have caught up with the Japanese. Who was winning?

It was time. He had to move on. Find the Americans. He could tell them that Yamashita was desperate, and had gone deeper into the hills.

Though by now, everything had probably changed.

Still, Zenji had to find his way out.

Leaving Abir was not easy. But when Zenji went through the motions of saying goodbye, the mountain people took no offense. They seemed to want whatever Zenji wanted.

"Thank you," Zenji said, his hand placed firmly on Abir's shoulder.

Abir understood, and clasped Zenji's shoulder in return. *"Ti ngarud,"* he said with a nod.

Within an hour Zenji had packed his pouch with what little he had, including the returned pistol—still loaded—a full canteen of water, and some food Abir had wrapped in leaves.

Zenji tried one more time. "Which way to a road?" He tried mimicking a winding roadway with his hands. "Road."

Abir understood.

Sort of.

He took Zenji to a path leading into the trees. *"Roaad."*

Zenji laughed and patted Abir's shoulder. "Of course."

At the edge of the jungle, Zenji turned back to glance one last time at the village and the mountain people who had been so kind to him. Twenty or thirty small men with red teeth squatted behind Abir, watching.

Abir raised a hand.

Zenji waved and headed into the jungle.

A few hours later, a burst of gunfire rattled in the near distance. It ended as abruptly as it had begun.

He turned to face where the sound had come from so he would know the direction.

He waited for more.

But that was it.

"This way," he said to himself, heading toward the battle, or whatever it had been.

Locate American forces.

Try not to get shot.

SHARP EDGE OF STEEL

He found only deeper, thicker jungle. He'd lost the path long ago. With no more sounds of war to guide him, and from what little he could see of the sun, he wasn't even sure of his direction.

He stood stone-still, listening.

Lost.

Fine. What's new? He would find his way out . . . eventually. Something or someone would stumble across his path. This green madness couldn't go on forever . . . unless he was traveling in circles.

That thought startled him. He'd have to figure out how to hold on to a single direction.

A week passed, then two. At least, that was what it seemed like. He wasn't sure of anything anymore.

Foraging for food wasn't easy. He'd grown weak, and was slowing down. Now he was eating leaves, grass, and bugs, as he'd seen the people in Abir's village do.

For water, he found trickling streams that had been reduced to mosquito-infested puddles. He lay on his stomach, pushed away the scum, and sipped what he could. So far, the water had not made him sick.

In the middle of one day he came to a rare clearing. He stopped and sat in a spill of wondrous sunlight, fingering the thin beard-like hair on his chin. His glasses were smudged, but he didn't care enough to clean them.

Had he been here before?

He sat for a long time, numb.

Before pushing on, he stretched out in the sun with his face to the sky and slept.

One afternoon he stumbled upon a running stream that snaked past the remains of an abandoned camp. Looked like a small platoon of soldiers had been there, and not too long ago.

He approached it cautiously.

"Oh," he whispered. "Oh, oh, oh!"

He squatted and picked up two small bags of rice. Japanese soldiers. Nearby, he found some powdered soy sauce and a few combat rations.

Why would they leave this behind? In Baguio they had been foraging in the jungle and eating off the streets. Where had this come from? Had they somehow been resupplied from the air?

Think later. Eat now.

He'd cook a small amount of rice.

Five matches. It was all he had left. He'd carefully preserved them.

He built a fire and boiled water from the stream with his mess kit. The rice cooked slowly. He watched the smoke rise into the trees.

His patience over how long it took to cook the rice was running thin. He gathered what dry leaves and twigs he could find and tossed them into the fire.

Thick smoke rose up.

He fanned the fire with his hand, trying to get it to spread.

Kaboom!

A thunderous barrage of artillery fire exploded all around him. A tree splintered and fell, just missing him.

He scrambled for cover.

More shells burst through the canopy, exploding, shattering trees, pulverizing dirt, vaporizing his fire.

Zenji grabbed his pouch and stumbled into the bushes. A shell exploded behind him. Another in front. A third almost on top of him. Dirt flying, branches shredding, everything blowing up.

He was suddenly flying.

He slammed into a tree and fell.

Then, nothing.

He awoke in utter darkness.

He had no idea how long he'd been unconscious. He tried to move. His arm worked. He touched his face. No blood.

He rose onto an elbow . . . and howled.

Pain shot through his side, low, near his hip. Like a blowtorch.

He fell back.

Don't touch it!

He lay in near delirium, panic welling.

What happened?

He remembered the abandoned camp. A fire. Rice cooking.

Explosions.

Trees shredding.

Flying, slamming into something.

He groaned.

The smoke. Someone had shot at the smoke.

Fear surged in a rush of sweat. He was wounded in a jungle where no one would ever find him.

He raised an arm, grateful that he could do that. He tried the other and his hopes soared. He wanted to sit, but feared the pain.

Slowly, lightly, he felt his body, and when his hand touched his side it came away wet.

Blood.

Gritting his teeth, he managed to sit. Again, he felt around, fingering his filthy, bloody, torn shirt. It was too dark to see anything. He wasn't sure he wanted to.

He pulled the material away and tenderly touched the wound. He could feel the sharp edge of steel. Shrapnel. The cut was deep, it seemed, and about three inches across.

He grimaced and ripped his shirt off. He bunched it up and pressed it over the wound. Slow the bleeding.

"This isn't good."

He squeezed his eyes shut and lay back, allowing the reality of having been wounded to settle in. He had to get out of this jungle.

Later, still lying on his back, he was amazed to see a blurry star blinking through the canopy.

Blurry?

My glasses!

Gone. Find them in the daylight.

Tears came to his eyes.

"Ma," he whispered, as if the word could cross the ocean, as if it would be heard, as if it—that one word—could make the world right.

"Ma."

Eventually, he slept.

When morning came he tried to get up.

"Ahhh!"

It took a while, but he managed to sit, the wound throbbing like the quickening heartbeat of fear.

Sweat rolled from his scalp across his cheek. Feverish.

"This is so bad."

The jungle was still.

No distant guns, no animals.

Birds. A few.

He reached up to rub his face, and when his hand fell back to the ground it hit his glasses. "Yes!"

He put them on. One lens was cracked. But he could see well enough. Not far away, his pouch lay, torn. There was a first-aid kit in it. Had to get it.

His legs worked, but he couldn't stand. He tried to roll over and get to his knees. But the pain was staggering.

With one hand holding the dirty shirt to his wound, he dragged himself over to the pouch. The first-aid kit had been pulverized. Amazingly, one of the two small bags of rice he'd found was still intact. He jammed it into his pants pocket.

Other than that, all that remained was a dented metal drinking cup and a piece of the kitchen knife. He gathered them. He didn't know where the pistol was.

The canteen had to be somewhere, unless it, too, had been blown to bits. He needed water to clean the wound.

No canteen.

But he did find the cap attached to a jagged piece of mangled metal.

53
UPSTREAM

Zenji slept, or maybe he had passed out. He didn't know.

Now, as he lay awake looking up at patches of blue sky through the canopy, the seriousness of his condition came back to him.

Got to move.

He dragged himself to his hands and knees, head spinning. The pain was staggering.

His body convulsed to retch, but nothing came out.

He crawled to a tree and sat with his back against it—dazed, half-conscious, his vision popping with colors.

Quiet jungle.

One birdsong, two.

Then an amazing thing happened: tears filled his eyes. They weren't tears of fear, but of the most unexpected sensation he could imagine in such desperation.

Peace.

He looked up. The world around him, the small patch of jungle, the pieces of sky, his hands, everything—all turned white, not just white as he knew white, but far more pure . . . and with that came stillness.

Fear ceased, and he floated in the peace that enveloped him.

The white light slowly turned back to blurry greens and blues as he became aware of the sound of flowing water.

A stream!

As he started to move, the pain in his side burned. He fingered the shrapnel, its sharp edge just under the skin. He tried to pinch it and pull it out. The pain nearly made him throw up.

Infection.

Get up.

Clean the wound.

Crawl!

With willpower he couldn't believe he had, Zenji pushed himself through the fire bellowing from his wound.

A strand of drool hung from his lips.

Hand. Knee. Hand.

Hope flickered.

The stream was less than twenty yards away.

It took him an hour to get there, dragging himself through twisted foliage and down a slight incline.

He didn't stop until he was submerged to his neck in the cold water. He drank like a horse, with greed, and when he was done he lay in the shallows on his back, the stream running over him.

After what seemed like hours, he struggled out to the dirt and slept.

When he awoke it was pitch-black. No stars shone through.
Alone.

The sound of the stream lulled him into a kind of oblivion, and soon hungry sharks swam parallel to a long sandy beach, tall coconut trees swirling in the wind, banyans wildly swaying, wind wailing, and seabirds soaring, diving, snapping fish from some unknown sea, and in one raging motion a wave of mynah birds swept down, landed on his chest, and with quick jabs, pecked out his eyes and ate them.

Zenji awoke with a gasp.

Fever.

He slept again in his sweat, and awoke sometime later in the earliest hint of day, visible only as a glow above the canopy.

He sat with effort.

Sleep had given him strength. This was good.

He dragged himself back into the stream and gently washed away the dirt-caked blood. The skin around the cut was red and swollen. The shrapnel had somehow worked its way up as he slept, the edge now much more visible.

It had to come out. He would not heal with it in there.

But all he had to extract it with was the piece of kitchen knife. He wiggled it out of his pocket and washed it in the water. What if the stream was polluted? He knew you should boil river water before drinking it.

Too late, anyway.

He studied the broken blade.

Do it.

Zenji Watanabe had never known true pain until now. First, he cut just under the surface, looking for a grip on the metal. Once he was able to pinch it, he began to pull.

He gritted his teeth and yanked.

"*Ahhhhh!*"

He stopped, panting, on the verge of passing out.

Now. One big yank and it's over.

"*Ahhhhhhhh!*"

He fainted, but came to when his head hit the water.

He sat breathing heavily, the shrapnel in his grip. Blood oozed from the wound and snaked away in the stream. A slab of flesh hung from the cut and Zenji fingered it back in, then pressed the gaping hole tight to slow the bleeding.

After a moment, he laughed and raised the shrapnel to the canopy. "You won't kill me! Nothing will kill me!"

Then he sobbed.

He lay by the stream for days, drinking its water and tending his wound. Eventually he could stand, and take a few steps, and finally, walk . . . slowly, with a limp.

But the cut was not healing.

Get moving, but stay near the river. Water means life.

He found a sturdy branch that was somewhat straight and broke it off to use as a cane.

He hobbled upstream.

Within minutes he discovered something that made him bend over and heave. *This* was why his wound had gotten worse.

He backed away from the bloated body of a Japanese soldier, writhing with maggots.

54
THE TRAP

Three weeks later, he was walking without the cane. His limp had gotten better, but he was still lost.

His wound began to heal once he'd started cleaning it upstream of the body. He kept it bandaged with mud and leaves and bark. He'd read about that in JROTC.

He ate only easily caught bugs and small translucent crayfish he captured in the stream. He ate them raw, eyeballs, legs, guts. He caught lots of them and stuck them in his pocket for later. They were chewy, and sweet, but if he kept them too long, they began to stink.

Still, he needed more.

Meat, if he could find it.

He would hunt.

That thought made him laugh. "Right. A hunter with a limp and a broken knife. I will hunt ants."

He laughed, loud.

He was losing it.

Who cared?

Where was the gunfire? He hadn't heard it in weeks. Had he gone so deep into the endless jungle that he was lost to all humans?

He stopped and listened for sounds, any sounds.

Quiet.

Must be closing in on evening.

Too bad his few remaining matches had gotten soaked in the river. He could cook the crayfish in his pocket, or maybe catch some fresh ones in the mud along the riverbank. Cooking them would at least break the monotony.

He no longer worried about smoke. He was on the moon, as far as that went.

So what had Abir done for fire?

Sticks.

Rub them together to make sparks fly. He wondered if he could do it. He could try.

As he limped along, he kept his eyes open. Besides the sticks, he'd need dry grass or leaves he could crumble between his hands.

For a while, the problem with following the river was mosquitoes. Soon they left him alone, and he was grateful for that. Probably my stink repulses them. They'd rather feed on a pig.

He snorted.

Near the end of the day he came upon a clearing. An outcropping of rock rose on one side. If it rained he would at least have some shelter.

He set up camp, making a bed of whatever softness he

could gather. He limped down to the stream for a drink, then came back to settle for the night. Too late for a fire. He'd do it tomorrow.

But what about the crayfish in his pockets? Some creature might wriggle in as he slept and eat them.

He ripped a piece of his ragged pant legs off and tightly wrapped the crayfish in it. He then wedged the bundle into a crack in the rock outcropping, where he hoped small night creatures couldn't reach it.

Looking up through the trees, the night sky astonished him. Stars! A whole universe of them. Billions.

"Wow," he whispered.

Stars gave him hope. People all over the world gazed at them, and that made him feel connected to something.

Other humans.

He wept.

When he awoke the next day, he found that the torn piece of pants had been taken from the crevice.

The crayfish were gone, every last one of them.

"Hey!" he yelled. *"Hey!"*

He gritted his teeth and tried to calm himself. Getting angry would do no good, and might even reopen his wound.

He sat and held his head in his hands.

A few minutes later he had a plan. He would catch whatever creature had stolen his stash and eat *it*!

Unless it was a poisonous snake.

All day long he looked for food, to eat and for bait. He found very little, which he ate. When he returned to his camp he sat and filled a new torn piece of his pants with dirt, adding in a few crayfish he managed to catch in the stream. For the smell.

He wondered if creatures were as easy to fool as humans.

He set the bundle back in the same crack and mulled over ideas for a trap. He was elated to find eight grains of rice in the seam of his pocket. They were damp and ruined, but still, perfect!

Cackling, he made a trail of them along the rock leading up to the bag of dirt and crayfish.

He fashioned a kind of platform out of sticks and propped it above the bundle on stilt legs. On the platform he placed a large rock, the heaviest that it would hold.

From the filthy, crumpled shirt that still bandaged his wound, he carefully removed enough threads to make a line about eight feet long. The threads were so aged and rotted that he worried they might break with even the slightest pull.

They'd have to do.

He tied one end of the line to a flimsy platform leg and stretched the rest of it back as far as it would go.

That night, he curled into a ball and waited.

He would listen. Sound would tell him when to pull the thread.

I can hear you tiptoe, little thief creature.

Zenji giggled, nearly ecstatic.

"Come, come."

He would not sleep until he pulled the leg out from under the platform, and he would only do that when he could hear the creature's feet scratching up to the bait.

But he dozed, and jolted awake a while later. "That wasn't smart," he mumbled.

He squinted at his moonlit trap. The trail of rice was still there.

This time he didn't lie down, but sat against a rock with his ear cocked.

Around an hour later, he heard the small scratchy sound of some creature closing in on the trap. He couldn't see it, but he could imagine it. Forward, stop. Forward, stop.

When the scratchy progress stopped, Zenji figured the creature was sniffing at the dirt bag and cussing its contents in animal language. Maybe a monkey?

He yanked on the thread.

The stone crashed down with a thump, rolling onto the ledge, off the face of rock, ending with a thump in the dirt.

Zenji scrambled over to it.

It would have to be a large thing to have survived that rock. He crept up to the trap.

The platform was broken in half, lying on the bag of dirt. There was nothing under it.

Zenji pursed his lips.

He got down on his knees, frantically searching the ground with his hands. He found the rock.

And the body.

He jerked his hand away at the weirdness of the warm, furry, dead thing. It had a long tail.

He could not identify it in the dark.

He wrapped it in fat leaves and set it under a small pile of rocks so some other creature wouldn't steal his food.

He went to sleep smiling.

In the morning, he would feast.

* * *

A rat.

Enormous. Sharp-toothed.

Zenji *hated* rats.

But it was meat.

He cut through the fur with his piece of knife and peeled the skin off the body. He wanted to cook it, but he couldn't start a fire with sticks.

He gave up trying and ate the thing raw.

It wasn't all that bad.

He was starving. He only had to forget what he was eating. He thought of it as pig. *Pig, pig, pig* ran through his mind as he chewed. *Ummm,* good pig. This is the best raw pig I've ever eaten.

He ate the whole thing, then lay on his stomach by the river and rinsed out his mouth.

He'd eaten dog.

Blood.

Bugs, grass, crayfish, and leaves.

Now rat.

I'm a savage, Ma.

He smiled, his full stomach brightening his mood.

The next day he found lice.

He ripped his pants off. They were all over his legs and chest, and his hair itched.

"Get off me!"

He sat in the stream and tried to wash them away. He laid down in the water and washed his hair. Those bloodsuckers were relentless. At least with the river he could scrub some of them away.

For a long time he lay on his back in the shallows at the edge of the stream with only his face above the surface. Drown, parasites, drown.

Finally, he got up and dried off in a patch of sun.

Keep going.

The sound of the stream comforted him as he followed it wherever it went. This is what his life had become: whatever, wherever, however.

What did it matter anymore?

You will come back to us, Zenji Watanabe.

Where had he heard that?

Keep going, keep going.

For days he followed the stream. He hadn't eaten well since the rat. Lice still feasted on him as he tried to sleep. And for the first time, his mind had started to play serious games with him. Sometimes he saw and truly believed things that were not there.

Abir, in the shadows.

Two boys, like wolves, staring.

A smoky ghost with no feet.

Nami, with three-inch fangs.

I should just stop.

Sit.

Die.

Just go to sleep and never wake up. It would be welcome. What a curious thought—just sit and die. Am I the one who thinks that thought? Or am I the one who thinks about thinking that thought?

He froze.

Voices!

People talking!

Oh, I know what this is. Zenji smiled. Death, creeping up to talk with him. The voices of dead people.

Death kept talking.

Death came closer.

Zenji's heart began to pound.

He scrambled to hide.

JUICY FRUIT

"**M**an, when I get home I'm going straight to the desert. I don't want to hear another mosquito sing to me for the rest of my life!"

English!

Zenji peeked through the bushes, breathless.

Six men.

None Japanese.

Americans? They looked it . . . but their uniforms were different. The insignias. He'd never seen anything like them. Who were these guys?

He could feel his hopes begin to soar. English. He hadn't heard a word of it in months. He started to stand but held back.

Be sure, be sure.

When he saw U.S. printed on their canteens he gasped. "It's them," he whispered. "It's them, it's them, it's *them*."

He closed his eyes and bowed his head. Thank you, he whispered to the God he believed had given him the will to keep on going.

Slowly, he stood.

No quick moves.

They would think he was a lost Japanese soldier, and he didn't want to be shot.

He raised his hands and stepped out into the open. "Don't shoot! Please . . . I'm an American . . . American."

The six men dropped to their knees and trained their weapons on him, stunned.

"Don't shoot. I'm unarmed."

Zenji got down and humbled himself. He was filthy, shirtless, with a blood-soaked bandage wrapped around his waist, and ripped and torn pants that were black with dirt and grime. His body was peppered with the shiny scars of cigarette burns.

"Don't move," one man said, approaching cautiously.

Zenji peeked up. The name printed on his uniform was Porter.

"You're no American."

Zenji kept his hands in view. "I'm G2, Military Intelligence. I was captured at Corregidor with General Wainwright and taken prisoner. They tortured me, then sent me to Manila to serve as houseboy to a Japanese colonel. I escaped in Baguio when Yamashita took his forces higher into the hills."

It was more than he'd said in months.

Porter glanced back at the other men. "Stand up," he said to Zenji. "You don't have to grovel."

Zenji struggled to his feet. Tell them what you know!

"Yamashita might still be around, I don't know. I got caught in artillery cross fire and was wounded."

Zenji peeled away the filth.

Porter winced. "What are all those marks on you?"

"Cigarette burns. Torture."

Porter eased up on the rifle. "You need medical attention, man."

"Yeah."

The five other men surrounded Zenji, studying him. One of them said, "You sure he's American? He don't look it."

"I'm American," Zenji pleaded. "From Honolulu. Military intelligence. G2. I need to find my unit. Colonel Olsten. I have information about where to find Yamashita."

Porter cocked his head. "*Find* him? You don't know?"

Zenji hesitated. "Know what?"

"We got Yamashita. The war's over. Ended in August."

"August? What month is it now?"

"Boy, you really have been lost. It's September 1945. We're out here looking for stragglers."

September? "The war's over? Who . . . we won?"

Porter grinned. "Those poor buggers sure didn't."

Zenji staggered.

Porter took his arm. "Come on, buddy. We got to get you some help."

He handed Zenji a canteen, and Zenji drank deeply.

"Keep it," Porter said.

It was like gold. A perfect canteen. There wasn't a scratch on it. "Thank you," he said. "Thank you."

Porter snorted. "You smell like a garbage dump, man."

Zenji tried to laugh he was so happy. He ended up coughing.

"Here," another man said. "Ain't food, but it's all I have."

Juicy Fruit gum.

Zenji looked at it as if he'd never seen a stick of gum in his life. He peeled away the wrapper and stuck the gum in his mouth.

Nothing.

In his entire life.

Had ever.

Tasted.

So.

Good.

Zenji grinned, and the man nodded.

"You get back to the regiment camp and get yourself a sweet California orange. Now, that's good!"

"Camp?"

Porter turned and lifted his chin. "A few miles thataway. Follow that trail. You'll see it." He looked up. "Getting late. Might have to stop and settle for the night before you get there. This place gets darker than dark."

"You're not going with me?"

Porter shook his head. "Gotta look for stragglers. Don't worry. Camp is close and easy to find. Just stay on the trail."

Zenji thanked them again, profusely.

"Approach with your hands up," Porter said. "You might scare somebody." He chuckled and waved to the other men. "Let's go!"

"Wait," Zenji said. "You can get lost in this place. How do you know where you're going?"

Porter pulled out a compass.

"Of course," Zenji said.

They gave him another canteen, some matches, and a clean undershirt and vanished into the jungle.

Zenji limped toward the camp.

September 1945.

That meant he was, what?

He stopped and thought about it. Really?

He was twenty-one years old now.

Unbelievable.

He'd gone only about two miles when night fell and he had to stop and spend one more night on the ground, right there on the trail. He wasn't moving from it. He would not get lost again.

He curled into a ball and used his crumpled, stinky, blood-caked shirt as a pillow. No way he was getting that pure white undershirt messed up.

"Ma," he whispered, tears of joy filling his eyes, "I'm coming home."

56
FIELD CAMP

The next morning he found the camp.

With one hand on his throbbing wound and the other raised in surrender, he called out.

"Don't shoot! I'm American!"

The startled sentry fumbled with his rifle when he saw Zenji coming toward him. He raised it to his cheek. "Down!" he shouted. "Get down! Now!"

Zenji obeyed, and the sentry ran toward him.

He forced Zenji onto his stomach, put a knee on his back, pinning him down and grinding his face into the dirt. "One move and I'll blow your brains out!"

"Please," Zenji pleaded. "I'm an American!"

"Shut up!"

The sentry turned and whistled for backup. Another guard came and the two of them dragged Zenji to his feet.

The second sentry turned his head to the side. "This Jap smells like a sewer!"

"I'm an American," Zenji said again. "I served with General Wainwright. I've been lost and—"

The first sentry jammed the butt of his rifle into Zenji's kidneys. "I said shut up!"

Zenji yelped and grabbed his back.

The two sentries frisked him. One of them found the knife blade and scoffed. "No wonder they ran."

The other sentry grunted. "You a deserter?"

"Hey," the first sentry said, nudging Zenji. "Why do you speak English?"

Zenji kept his mouth shut. He needed to talk to people with bigger brains.

The sentries herded him toward the regiment camp. "I want to see your commanding officer," Zenji said.

"How about a nice soft bed with feather pillows, too?"

Zenji didn't respond.

Men stared at him as the sentries marched him through camp to an army tent, where he was forced to sit cross-legged on the dirt floor. One sentry remained with him while the other went to find an officer.

Master Sergeant Gage ducked into the tent twenty minutes later. He looked Zenji over. "Stand."

Zenji struggled up.

"You say you're American?"

"Zenji Watanabe, from Honolulu. G2. United States Military Intelligence Corps, badge number B-12, code name Bamboo Rat."

Gage eyed him.

"Contact Colonel Olsten," Zenji added. "He'll confirm that."

"We doing undercover work in the jungle now?"

"I was on Corregidor when it fell and I was captured." He pointed to the cigarette scars. "They threw me in a POW camp and tortured me, trying to get me to admit I was a spy. I told them nothing. They kept me there for a year, I guess, and finally gave up on me. They would have executed me, but because I speak Japanese and English, they forced me to work for them in Manila. Colonel Fujimoto. When they retreated to Baguio I escaped. Got lost in the jungle, for months. Some of your men found me yesterday . . . Porter . . . Porter sent me here."

Gage stared at Zenji.

"Get this man cleaned up," he said after a long moment. "Take him to first aid and have them look at that wound, then give him something to eat, a shower, and something to wear. Stay with him while I check this out. If he tries to run, shoot him."

As gruesome as Zenji's shrapnel wound looked, the medic told him he'd done a good job with what he'd had to work with. "Amazing. You're a tough son of a gun. Gonna leave a nasty scar, though."

"I got a collection of scars."

"I see."

They gave him a set of khakis, a hot field shower, fed him, and let him rest on a cot. It was the most luxurious two hours of his life.

A private came to escort Zenji to the commanding officer,

a major. His name was Connelly, and he was extremely apologetic.

"We spoke with a field office near Manila and got your story, pretty much as you told it to Master Sergeant Gage. You were listed as missing. They were amazed that you were still alive! They're sending a jeep to pick you up in the morning."

Connelly sat back and crossed his arms. "You say you actually saw Yamashita?"

"Yes, sir, briefly."

"And what was this man like?"

Zenji thought a moment. "Honorable, sir, unlike some of the other Japanese officers. He was protective of his men."

The major nodded. "In war you see the best and the worst in people."

"Yes. You do."

The next morning a jeep carrying two lieutenants arrived. They greeted Zenji like a long-lost hero, and for the first time in months Zenji allowed himself to feel safe.

To feel happy.

He could only nod.

That night, Zenji did not eat dog, bugs, or rat.

But that would have been preferable to the shock that awaited.

57
A GLIMMER

Manila was a city of rubble.

The place Zenji had come to love had been brought to its knees. While he'd hobbled around lost, Manila had suffered the worst urban street fighting in the Pacific War. It had lasted for over a month and left the city in ruins.

Even so, optimism wove through the streets, alleys, neighborhoods, and communities that edged the rivers and bay. A heartbeat remained, growing stronger.

By now the victory celebrations had ended.

The city had turned to rebuilding.

As they drove, Zenji could hardly take it all in. What a waste it had all been, the killing, the destruction. Had it really been necessary?

Of course.

Japan had lost way more than it ever gained, and innocent people throughout the Pacific had suffered for it.

Then his driver told him about suffering of unimaginable proportions. Hiroshima and Nagasaki had been flattened by two horrific atomic bombs. The alien shock had finally brought the war in the Pacific to an end.

Zenji could not grasp such destruction. Japan was still the country where his parents were born, and it was nearly as important to him as his own.

All those innocent people.

Why, why, why had so much gone so wrong?

Back at headquarters, Zenji looked for time to be alone, walking, sitting, dreaming, meditating. He also tried to find out where Freddy and Benny had ended up, and Esteban Navarro. But there was no credible information available, so he left messages with people he knew to contact him if something came up.

He prayed that they were safe.

Alive.

It was so amazing. To breathe, to think and feel.

He needed strength, and hope.

And he needed to call home.

But there was a problem—his mother spoke only Japanese, and it was forbidden to speak Japanese on calls in the Pacific. He could speak to his mother only through Colonel Blake, and Colonel Blake had to find a translator because he couldn't understand Ma.

It took two days, but people at HQ and the colonel worked it out.

Zenji stood in a hallway, the phone on a small table. "Ma,"

he said in English, because he had to. She didn't understand, but she could hear his voice. "I'm okay, Ma. I'm coming home soon."

On the other end of the line he could hear his mom speaking through tears to the translator, and the translator to Colonel Blake.

Colonel Blake came on the line. "Zenji, my God, we're overjoyed! Your mother is too shocked to speak, and happy, very, very happy. We'd thought that you hadn't made it. They told us you'd been captured and were missing, and could even be dead."

"Yeah, it was . . . something."

"We're all so proud of you, son."

"Sir, can you tell Ma I'm fine? And that I'll be home soon, I hope."

"I will, and don't worry about your mother. We'll take care of her. Hey, your sister wants—"

"Zenji?" Aiko was sobbing.

Tears flooded Zenji's eyes. "Aiko."

"You're alive!"

"I'm fine. Oh, it's so good to hear your voice. Henry taking good care of you? Are you staying out of trouble?"

"I'm older now. You've been gone four years. Four years! I don't do trouble anymore."

Zenji laughed. "And I'm older, too."

If she only knew. Would he ever tell her what he'd been through? He would never tell *anyone*! He'd bury it deep.

"When are you coming home?"

"Don't know. They got me doing some work here, translating. . . . I think they're going to use me in court, too. War crimes. That's the rumor."

"Sounds bad."

"Yeah. . . . Hey, where's Henry?"

"He couldn't get off for a phone call, can you believe it? Not even for this. He said you're a hero."

"He did?"

"He has a nice girlfriend. Yasuko. He's the head of his department now."

"Bound to happen. He works hard."

"Hey, remember Nami and Ken? They're going to be *sooo* happy to hear that you're coming home!"

Zenji smiled.

"I got a puppy. Her name is Ipo."

"Sweetheart," Zenji said, translating the Hawaiian.

"She likes papayas."

"Papayas! Boy, do I miss those!"

"I'll fill your room with them."

They laughed.

There was a long moment of silence. He couldn't begin to describe his emotions.

"Hey," he finally said. "Make sure Ma knows I'm really okay, and that I'll be home soon."

"Yeah, I will."

Zenji leaned his forehead on the wall. "Write to me every day, and I'll write to you."

"I will . . . but, Zenji?"

"Yeah?"

"Wait."

He waited.

A few seconds passed.

"Zenji? Hello? Are you there?"

A pause.

"Mina?"

"It's true," she said. "You *are* alive. Our prayers . . ." She was sobbing.

He said nothing. He couldn't. He was no longer the person she'd known. He was crazy, maybe. He'd been through too much.

"You don't have to say anything," she said. "We're . . . we're so happy, Zenji. I'll just give the phone to—"

"No . . . please."

Silence.

"It's okay, Zenji," she said.

"When I come home . . . will you . . . will you be there with my family?"

"Of course."

After he said goodbye to everyone, he hung up and stood dazed until someone nudged him. "Hey, buddy. Mind if I use the phone?"

After far too little recuperation, Zenji was debriefed, which meant he sat with two army interrogators who asked a thousand questions about where he'd been and what he'd done. Unbelievably, they questioned his loyalty, due to his time serving Colonel Fujimoto.

"Why would I tell you about that if I had something to hide? I was a prisoner. I was forced to work for him."

The men scribbled notes.

Zenji inquired about Colonel Olsten and General Wainwright. Surely they would vouch for him. But they'd been sent stateside.

Zenji gritted up. His questioners never had a chance. After what he'd been through, Zenji could stand up to any interrogation.

Plus, he was innocent.

Eventually, he was assigned to the Apprehension and Interrogation Division of the War Crimes Commission.

The rage and hatred that had built up inside him at his torturers was still there, made worse every time he saw his ugly scars.

He tried not to think. To focus on going home, being with his family again. He hated that he hated. But how could he *not* hate?

There was a way he could start.

With two men.

He found their names going through the records of all U.S. POW camps. They were in two different locations.

With the authority he'd been given by the War Crimes Commission, Zenji had them brought to Manila: Colonel Nakamichi from the Kempeitai, and John Jones.

Somehow he didn't hate the guards who had done the actual torturing. They'd been following orders.

On the day of confrontation, Zenji had Jones and Nakamichi placed in an interrogation room. He let them sit awhile, wondering what the interaction between the two men might be like.

He stood outside in the hall with a guy named Maeda, an interpreter he'd brought along to help disguise his own identity. Maeda was a Los Angeles Japanese, a couple of years younger than he was.

Zenji put on a pair of dark glasses. Was he *really* ready for this? Was this the way?

Yes.

As much as possible, it would end here.

Today.

Zenji looked up.

Maeda's eyes were steady. "Can't wait."

Zenji nodded. "Let's go."

Two guards stood outside the door. Zenji followed Maeda in.

Nakamichi and John Jones sat apart, Jones slumped in his metal chair, gazing at the floor. The colonel sat erect, staring straight ahead. They both wore white T-shirts and khaki pants, the colonel stripped of rank. Both looked thinner, older.

Zenji sat in the corner.

Maeda took charge, at first simply staring at the prisoners.

The colonel never took his gaze from the wall.

"I'm not supposed to be here," Jones said. "You guys have it all wrong. I'm an *American*. Why won't anyone listen to me? What have I done? I *demand* that you tell me! I have rights!"

Nakamichi didn't twitch.

Zenji knew the colonel couldn't understand what Jones was saying, but he could probably sense the nature of it.

Maeda stared at Jones.

Jones could not hold his gaze, an obvious tell. Zenji felt his blood begin to boil. This was the man who'd gotten Captain Thomson executed! He started to rise, ready to strangle him.

No . . . no.

He eased back down.

Jones saw Zenji looking. "Great. Two Japs."

Zenji gripped the edge of the chair.

"We're looking for someone," Maeda said to Jones. "His name is Zenji Watanabe. Ever heard of him?"

"No."

Maeda's eyes were like ice picks.

Jones turned away.

"Zenji Watanabe wo sagasiteiru," Maeda repeated to Colonel Nakamichi. *"Zenji Watanabe wo shitteruka?"*

Nakamichi turned to look at Maeda. Then he glanced over at Zenji.

He looked back at Maeda and shook his head.

Zenji stood.

Nakamichi and Jones turned toward him.

He walked closer. Taking his time.

Slowly, he removed his dark glasses.

He saw the instant of recognition in each man's eyes.

Jones's jaw sagged. He'd just seen his death. Zenji would identify him as a traitor. He would be tried and executed.

Nakamichi stood.

Maeda stepped closer to Zenji, glanced over to the guards at the door.

Zenji held up his hand, reading the horror in Nakamichi's eyes.

Guilt. Shame. Sorrow.

The colonel bowed deeply, then prostrated himself on the floor and begged for forgiveness, begged to be put to death. *"Koroshite kudasai. Watashi niwa ikiru kachinado nainda."*

In that moment, the war ended for Zenji.

The colonel was so ashamed he'd asked to be executed immediately. He did not deserve to live.

The colonel's shame and noble request snuffed the vengeance out of Zenji. He could only feel as one with this man in this moment. There was no separation.

The culmination of Zenji's war: sadness, deeper than any he'd ever known. No one had escaped.

"It's over," Zenji whispered.

In his heart he forgave Colonel Nakamichi.

For Jones he felt nothing.

At the door, he turned to look at the two men. "I was the Bamboo Rat," he said.

He nodded in gratitude to Maeda and left the room.

Outside in the sun, he breathed the rich tropical air. So much in his world had to be repaired. He needed to restore his faith in humankind, to pick himself up and move on. It was time. Move on, and thrive.

He sighed and headed through the broken city to the bay. All he wanted right now was to see the sun sparkling on the water.

And go home.

58

YELLOW GINGER

A huge crowd cheered as the ship arrived, people waving and jumping. Zenji whistled at the sight of all the banners and flags and signs, and enough flower leis to cover the deck of an aircraft carrier.

There—Ma and Henry! He waved. He didn't see Aiko, but Colonel Blake was there with Tosh and Naomi, who were both yelling up to him.

Zenji waved both arms, a grin squeezing the edges of his face.

Where was Aiko? And Mina? They weren't with his family.

He pushed his way down the gangway. "Ma!"

"Zenji!"

He ran up, lifted her off the ground, and swung her around. He doubted anyone had ever done that to her.

Ma was too overwhelmed to speak, but she refused to let

Zenji go, gripping his shirt the whole time he hugged every-one else.

"Colonel!"

"I'm so proud of you, Zenji, and so relieved!"

Zenji hugged Tosh and Naomi.

"Big brother." Zenji grabbed Henry.

Henry grinned. "Still as skinny as ever, I see. Man, I'm glad you're home."

"You and me both. Where's Aiko?"

Henry turned to look behind him.

Aiko stood alone. Zenji was shocked to see a somber young woman with long shining hair.

"Go," Henry said.

Ma let go of his shirt.

"Aiko, Aiko," he said, approaching her cautiously. "Look at you! All grown up! You're beautiful!"

She threw herself at him, weeping. "I thought you were dead!"

"Little sister!" He held her close. "My Aiko. I'm still here, as you can see. Why are you over here by yourself?"

"Because of this!"

Aiko pulled away and Mina stepped out from behind her.

"I told you I'd be here." She put a yellow ginger lei around his neck and hugged him.

Zenji held on to Aiko and Mina, the ginger smelling sweeter than anything he could ever remember.

I'm safe. I'm free. All will be well.

"Hey, Mina," he said. "You still like Benny Goodman?"

She laughed through tears and hugged him again.

Everyone crowded around, touching Zenji.

"Come," Ma said. "We go home."

AUTHOR'S NOTE

This novel was inspired by the extraordinary story of Hawaii-born Richard Sakakida's military intelligence service in the Philippines during World War II. It is a fictional account of some of his exploits; I invented the characters, the dialogue, and many of the events.

Richard Sakakida was awarded the Legion of Merit, the Bronze Star, and two Commendation Medals, and was inducted into the Military Intelligence Hall of Fame. His fascinating memoir is called *A Spy in Their Midst: The World War II Struggle of a Japanese-American Hero* (as told to Wayne Kiyosaki).

The character of Freddy Kimura was inspired by the military intelligence service of Arthur Komori, and the civilian experiences of Clarence Yamagata inspired the character of Benny Suzuki. Sakakida, Komori, and Yamagata were Japanese Americans from Hawaii. The character of Esteban Navarro was inspired by Ernest Tupas, a World War II Filipino resistance leader. The character Maeda was based on one of roughly six thousand Japanese Americans who served against Japan in the Military Intelligence Service during World War II.

Abir's language comes from my research into the indigenous Ibaloi language, which is slowly disappearing in favor of more commonly used languages.

GLOSSARY

HAWAIIAN

haole: Foreigner, Caucasian.

IBALOI

Mayatya davi: An evening greeting.

Nganto y ngagan mo?: What is your name?

Ti ngarud: Goodbye.

Toy edapo-an mo?: Where are you coming from?

JAPANESE

Ashiga tsukanaiyouni musubi agero: Bind him! Raise him off his feet.

Deteikimasen: He refuses to leave.

Haire: Go.

Ho-su mottekoi: Get the hose.

Ieni wa inaiyo: Not home.

Isuwo mottekoi: Get me a chair.

Kanji: Characters used to write in Japanese.

Koitsuwo sotoni tsureteitte korose: Take this man out and shoot him.

Koitsuwo utsu jyunbi wo siro: Get ready to shoot this man.

Kokowa darega sikitteiruka kike: Ask who's in charge here.

Kono kitanai mizuni haitte sono kitanai karadawo arae:
Get in! Clean your disgusting body!

Konohito: He's in charge.

Koroshite kudasai. Watashi niwa ikiru kachinado nainda:
Please kill me. I don't deserve to live.

Mou ii: Enough!

mushi: Worms.

Naine: Not likely.

Namae to kaikyu-wa?: Your name and rank?

Namae wa?: Your name?

Nugase!: Strip him!

omae: You.

Omaewa hanasuna: You are not to speak.

ro-pu: Rope.

Rouya ni tsurete kaere: Take him back to his cell.

Samonaito zenin utsuzo: If they don't leave, we will shoot
them.

Shizuka dattakara: You were so quiet.

Susume!: Go! Move!

Tsurete ike!: Take him away!

Ugoke!: Move!

Yamero!: Stop!

Zenin tsureteike: Get them all out of here.

Zenji Watanabe wo sagasiteiru?: Do you know Zenji
Watanabe?

RESOURCES

Belote, James H., and William M. Belote. *Corregidor: The Saga of a Fortress*. New York: Harper & Row Publishers, 1967.

Fujita, Frank. *Foo: A Japanese-American Prisoner of the Rising Sun*. Denton, TX: University of North Texas Press, 1993.

Hawaii Nisei History Editorial Board. *Japanese Eyes, American Heart: Personal Reflections of Hawaii's World War II Nisei Soldiers*. Honolulu: University of Hawaii Press, 1998.

Kimura, Yukiko. *Issei: Japanese Immigrants in Hawaii*. Honolulu: University of Hawaii Press, 1988.

McNaughton, James. *Nisei Linguists: Japanese Americans in the Military Intelligence Service During World War II*. Washington, DC: Department of the Army, 2006.

Odo, Franklin S. *No Sword to Bury: Japanese Americans in Hawai'i During World War II*. Philadelphia: Temple University Press, 2004.

Saiki, Patsy Sumie. *Ganbare! An Example of Japanese Spirit*. Honolulu: Mutual Publishing, 2004.

Sakakida, Richard. *A Spy in Their Midst: The World War II Struggle of a Japanese-American Hero*. As told to Wayne Kiyosaki. Lanham, MD: Madison Books, 1995.

Smurthwaite, David. *The Pacific War Atlas 1941–1945*. New York: Facts on File, Inc., 1995.

Yenne, Bill. *Rising Suns: The Japanese American GIs Who Fought for the United States in World War II*. New York: Thomas Dunne Books, 2007.

ACKNOWLEDGMENTS

Very special thank-yous to Takako Kyo Stec for providing Japanese translations; to Drusilla Tanaka for her support and constant ability to put me in touch with valuable resources; to Mark Matsunaga for his critical military eye; to Victor Ramon G. Marfori, Jr., for sharing his knowledge of the war in the Philippines; and to other early readers Monica White, Randi Abel, and Samantha Rodan.

Thanks to my outstanding team at Random House Children's Books: Wendy Lamb, my good friend and editor from day one of my writing career (who makes this writer reach down deep for his very best—*mahalo nui loa* for that); Dana Carey, kindhearted assistant editor; and Colleen Fellingham and Heather Lockwood Hughes, amazing, amazing copy editors. Thanks to Kate Gartner for the thrilling new Prisoners of the Empire cover art and to Trish Parcell for the fine interior design and map, and to my talented marketing professionals: John Adamo, Judith-the-Great Haut, Lydia Finn, Kim Lauber, Lisa Nadel, and the ever-hardworking Adrienne Waintraub.

A very special thank-you to my supportive friends and family— you mean the world to me. And finally, a ginormous thank-you to the heroes: teachers, librarians, parents, and young readers everywhere who are out there keeping books alive and well. *Mahalo nui loa!*